Lord

Translations

SALZWASSER
VERLAG

Lord Lyttelton, W.E. Gladstone

Translations

Reprint of the original, first published in 1863.

1st Edition 2022 | ISBN: 978-3-37500-334-0

Verlag (Publisher): Salzwasser Verlag GmbH, Zeilweg 44, 60439 Frankfurt, Deutschland
Vertretungsberechtigt (Authorized to represent): E. Roepke, Zeilweg 44, 60439 Frankfurt, Deutschland
Druck (Print): Books on Demand GmbH, In de Tarpen 42, 22848 Norderstedt, Deutschland

TRANSLATIONS

BY

LORD LYTTELTON

AND

THE RIGHT HON. W. E. GLADSTONE.

SECOND EDITION.

LONDON:

1863.

CONTENTS.

TRANSLATIONS BY LORD LYTTELTON.

INTO GREEK.

INTO LATIN.

TRANSLATIONS
BY THE RIGHT HON. W. E. GLADSTONE.

FROM THE GREEK.

CONTENTS.

TRANSLATIONS

BY

LORD LYTTELTON.

Comus.

THE star, that bids the shepherd fold,
Now the top of heaven doth hold;
And the gilded car of day
His glowing axle doth allay
In the steep Atlantic stream;
And the slope Sun his upward beam
Shoots against the dusky pole,
Pacing toward the other goal
Of his chamber in the east.
Meanwhile welcome joy and feast,
Midnight shout and revelry,
Tipsy dance and jollity.
Braid your locks with rosy twine
Dropping odours, dropping wine.
Rigour now is gone to bed,
And Advice with scrupulous head;
Strict Age and sour Severity,
With their grave saws in slumber lie.
We that are of purer fire
Imitate the starry quire,
Who in their nightly watchful spheres
Lead in swift round the months and years.

'ΑΣΤΗΡ, ποιμέσι καιρὸς ἐναύλου,
κατέχει μέσσον φαιδρὸς Ὄλυμπον·
τέγγει δ' ἄξονα τὸν πυριθαλπῆ
ῥείθροις πρηνέσιν Ἀτλαντείοις
δίφρος ὁ Φοίβου χρυσεόκυκλος·
πόλον ἠέλιος πρὸς ἀμαυρὸν
λεχρίαν ἀκτῖν' ἐπάνω βάλλων
εἰς ἀντίπορον τέρμονα κοίτας
τὰς ἠώας μεταβαίνει.
χαῖρ' οὖν Θαλία, χαῖρ' Εὐφροσύνα,
κῶμοί τε, βοά θ' ἁ μεσονύκτιος,
οἰνοπλάνητόν τ' ὄρχημ' ἄπονον·
πλέκετ' ἐν ῥοδίῳ πλέγματι χαίταν
χρίσμασιν ὑγρὰν, ὑγρὰν Βρομίῳ·
νῦν γε τὸ Σεμνὸν κατακοιμᾶται,
τό τε Νουθεσίας ὄμμα περίσσοφρον·
ἀπαράμυθον[1] δ' εὕδει Γῆρας,
χἁ Σωφροσύνα, δριμεῖα θεὰ,
σοφίαν θρυλοῦσα ματαίαν.
ἡμεῖς δὲ φλογὸς τᾶς ἁγνοτέρας
ἀστεροειδῆ
ζηλοῦμεν χορὸν, οἱ παννυχίοις
ἄγρυπνα κύκλοις περιτελλομένων
ἐτέων φυγάδας μῆνας ἄγουσιν.

[1] Vide Blomf. ad *Æsch. Prom.* 193.

The sounds and seas with all their finny drove
Now to the moon in wavering morrice move:
And on the tawny sands and shelves
Trip the pert faeries and the dapper elves:
By dimpled brook and fountain brim
The wood-nymphs, decked with daisies trim,
Their merry wakes and pastimes keep.
What hath night to do with sleep?
Night hath better sweets to prove,
Venus now wakes, and wakens love:
Come, let us our rites begin;
'Tis only daylight that makes sin,
Which these dun shades will ne'er report,
Hail, goddess of nocturnal sport,
Dark-veiled Cotytto! to whom the secret flame
Of midnight torches burns; mysterious dame,
That ne'er art called, but when the dragon womb
Of Stygian darkness spits her thickest gloom,

λιμένες, πορθμοί τ', αἰολόφυλοι τ'
ἰχθύες ἤδη μαρμαρυγαῖσιν
δίαν τιμῶσι Σελάναν·
κατὰ δὲ ξούθους ἁλὸς αἰγιαλοὺς
σκιρτᾷ λάλιον μορμολύκειον,
ῥαδινά τ' ἔμπουσα χορεύει.
παρὰ μειδώντων
νάματα κρουνῶν ἄκρα τε χείλη,
Δρυάδες, κομψὰν κόσμον ἔχουσαι
βαλλίδα, τερπνοῖς παίγνι' ἄγουσιν
κώμοις ἱλαραί·
νὺξ δέ μοι ὕπνῳ τὶ σὺ κοινωνεῖς;
νὺξ μέγ' ἀμείνω τέρψιν παρέχει·
Κύπρις ἐγερθεῖσ' υἱὸν ἐγείρει·
σπεύδετε δ'· ἡμὶν ἐς ὄργια καιρός·
μόνον ἐκφαίνει φῶς ἀλιτήμονα·
ταῦτα δὲ κευθμὼν
σκοτόεις οὔ πως ἀποδείξει.
χαῖρε μελάμπεπλος ἐν νυκτερίνοις
παίγμασι δαῖμον, χαῖρε, Κοτυττώ·
σοὶ πῦρ δᾴδων πάννυχον αἴθει
κρυφίων, δέσποιν' ἄφατος, κληθεῖσ'
ὁπότε Στυγίας ὁ δρακοντώδης
νεφέλας γαστὴρ καταπυκνοτάταν
ἔπτυσεν ὄρφναν,

And makes one blot of all the air:
Stay thy cloudy ebon chair,
Wherein thou ridest with Hecat, and befriend
Us thy vowed priests, 'till utmost end
Of all thy dues be done, and none left out;
Ere the babbling eastern scout,
The nice morn, on the Indian steep
From her cabin'd loop-hole peep,
And to the tell-tale sun descry
Our conceal'd solemnity.
Come, knit hands, and beat the ground
In a light fantastic round.

MILTON.

ἀέρα χραίνων κηλῖδι μιᾷ·
δίφρους Ἑκάτᾳ σοί θ' ἅμα κοινοὺς
ἐβένου παῦσον ζοφόεντος,
σοῦ δ' εὐόρκους ἱερεῖς ἡμᾶς
βλέψον πρευμενὲς, ἕς τ' ἂν τελετὰς
πάντως πάσας σοὶ τελέσωμεν,
πρίν γ' ἐξ ἑδρῶν λαλὸν ἠφων
φύλακ' ἐν κορυφαῖς Ἰνδῶν ἁπαλὰν
Ἠριγενείαν, σκοπιάζουσαν
τῆλ' ἐκ θυρίδος μυχόθεν κοίλας,
ἀθυρογλώττῳ δεῖξαι Φοίβῳ
τάδ' ἀποῤῥήτων ὄργια θεσμῶν.
ἄγετ' οὖν, φιλίας ἅπτετε χεῖρας,
καὶ ποδὶ κούφῳ
πολυδαίδαλα πλήττετε γαῖαν.

L. 1832.

Sweet Echo.

SWEET Echo, sweetest nymph, that liv'st unseen
Within thy aery shell,
By slow Meander's margent green,
And in the violet-embroidered vale,
Where the love-lorn nightingale
Nightly to thee her sad song mourneth well:
Canst thou not tell me of a gentle pair
That likest thy Narcissus are?
O! if thou have
Hid them in some flowery cave,
Tell me but where,
Sweet queen of parley, daughter of the sphere!
So may'st thou be translated to the skies,
And give resounding grace to all heaven's harmonies.

MILTON.

Ἀχώ, κλῦθί μοι, Ἀχώ,   στροφή.
νυμφάων ἀγαυοτάτα,
κρυπτὸν ἀέριον σκάφος
ναίουσ', ἢ χλοερὰν πλάκα
Μαιάνδρου πάρ' ἀκύμονος,
βάσσας ἢ κάτ' ἰοδνεφεῖς,
ὅπου θ' ἁ δυσέρως πάννυχ'
ἀηδὼν μέλος οἰκτρὸν
καλῶς σοὶ καταθρηνεῖ·
λίσσομαι, ἀβράν μοι,
κούρα, φράζε συνωρίδα,
ποῦ ναίει, μάλα τῷ σῷ   ἀντιστρ.
Ναρκίσσῳ δέμας ἐμφερής·
εἰ δ' ἔκρυψας ἐν ἄνθεσι
σπηλαίου τινος, ἀλλά μοι
εἴποις ποῦ ποτε, φιλτάτα
φεῦ δέσποιν' ὀάρου θεά,
πρόφρασσ', οὐρανόπαι. κεὶς πο-
λὸν οὕτω μεταναστᾶσ',
Ὀλύμποιο μελάθρων
εὐκέλαδον πάσῃ
δοίης ἁρμονίᾳ χάριν.

L. 1833.

The Sacrifice.

Choose the darkest part o' th' grove,
Such as ghosts at noon-day love.
Dig a trench, and dig it nigh
Where the bones of Laius lie:
Altars raised of turf or stone
Will the infernal Pow'rs have none.
Answer me, if this be done?
'Tis done.

Is the sacrifice made fit?
Draw her backward to the pit:
Draw the barren heifer back;
Barren let her be and black.
Cut the curled hair that grows
Full betwixt her horns and brows:
And turn your faces from the sun.
Answer me, if this be done?
'Tis done.

Pour in blood and bloodlike wine,
To mother earth and Proserpine:
Mingle milk into the stream:
Feast the ghosts that love the steam.
Snatch a brand from funeral pile:
Toss it in to make them boil:
And turn your faces from the sun.
Answer me, if this be done?
'Tis done.

DRYDEN.

Ἄγ' οὖν, σκοτεινὸν ἐξερευνήσας μυχὸν,
οἷον μεσημβρινοῖσιν ἐν χρόνοις φιλεῖ
εἴδωλ' ἐνοικεῖν, Λαΐου πεσήμασι
παρ' ὀστίνοισι σκάπτε μοι τάφρου βάθος.
οὐ γάρ τι χλωροῖς οὐδὲ λαΐνοις ποτὲ
χαίρουσι βωμοῖς οἵ γε νέρτεροι Θεοί.
λέγ' εἰ πέπρακται ταῦτα;
Πᾶν καλῶς ἔχει.

ἆρ' ηὐτρέπισται πάνθ' ὅσα σφαγῆς ἔχει;
τὴν στεῖραν οὖν ὄπισθεν εἰς τάφρον χρεὼν
μόσχον καθέλκειν· τοῦτο δ' εὖ φύλασσ', ὅπως
στεῖραν τε καὶ μέλαιναν αἱμάξεις χεροῖν.
ἔπειτα πλεκτὰς δεῖ σ' ἀποθρίσαι τρίχας,
ἅσπερ κεράτων ὀμμάτων τ' ἔχει μέσας.
τρέπεσθε δ' ὄψιν πᾶς ἀνὴρ ἀφ' ἡλίου.
λέγ' εἰ πέπρακται ταῦτα;
Πᾶν καλῶς ἔχει.

ἀλλ' αἵματ' ἐγχεῖν αἵμασίν τε προσφερὲς
οἴνου γάνος μέμνησο, παμμήτωρ δὲ Γῆ
δῶρον τόδ' ἱερὸν ἥ τε Περσέφασσ' ἔχοι·
προσθὲς δὲ ταῖς ῥοαῖσι συγκραθὲν γάλα,
ἵν' ἀτμίσιν χαίροντες οἱ κεκμηκότες
θαλίαν ἔχωσιν· ἐκ δέ του νεκρῶν πυρᾶς
ἀφαρπάσας σὺ δαλὸν εἰς τάφρον βάλε,
ὅπως τὸ σύμπαν κάρτ' ἀναζέσει φλογί.
τρέπεσθε δ' ὄψιν πᾶς ἀνὴρ ἀφ' ἡλίου.
λέγ' εἰ πέπρακται ταῦτα;
Πᾶν καλῶς ἔχει.

L. 1837.

The Lotos-eaters.

"Courage!" he said, and pointed toward the land:
"This mountain wave will roll us shoreward soon."
In the afternoon they came unto a land,
In which it seemed always afternoon.
All round the coast the languid air did swoon,
Breathing like one that hath a weary dream.
Full-faced above the valley stood the moon;
And like a downward smoke, the slender stream
Along the cliff to fall and pause and fall did seem.

A land of streams! some, like a downward smoke,
Slow-dropping veils of thinnest lawn, did go:
And some thro' wav'ring lights and shadows broke,
Rolling a slumb'rous sheet of foam below.

MEMORIÆ
HENRICI DRURY
MUSIS AMICI
QUO FAUTORE
NUGÆ HUJUSMODI NONNULLÆ
QUIBUS HORAS
SEU TRISTES SIVE VACUAS
FEFELLERAT
IN PUBLICUM PRODIERUNT
NUPER EHEU PEREMPTI
D. D.
L

“ Θάρσος,” ἔφη· και χεῖρας ὀρεξάμενος ποτὶ γαῖαν,
ηὔχετ’ ἐπ’ ἀκροπόλου ταχέως μάλα κύματος ἥξειν.
ἑσπέριοι δ’ ἤκουσιν,[1] ὅθ’ ἕσπερος ἀΐδιός τις
φαίνετ’· ἀλύεσκεν δ’ ἀκτὴν πέρι νήνεμος ἀὴρ,
δύσπνοον ὡς βρίζοντος ὄναρ· μεγαλωστὶ σελήνη
στῆ καθύπερθε νάπης· ἐπὶ δ’ οὔρεος, ἠΰτε καπνὸς,
στάζε τε καὶ λῆγεν καὶ στάζεν ἀμοιβαδὶς ὕδωρ.

ῥείθρων ἔβρυε γῆ· πρηνὴς τὰ μὲν ἠΰτε καπνὸς,
ἠὲ λίνου ποτ’ ἄωτος, ἄνωθεν λεπτότατα ψῆ·[2]
τῶν δ’ ἄπο, μαρμαρυγὰς μεταμειβομένην τε δι’ ἀχλὺν,
κωφὸν[3] παφλάζοντα, κατέκλυζ’ οἶδματ’ ἄβυσσον.

[1] *Od.* IX. 336. [2] Brunck. *ad Soph. Trach.* 678.
[3] *Il.* XIV. 16.

They saw the gleaming river seaward flow
From th' inner land: far off, three mountain-tops,
Three silent pinnacles of aged snow,
Stood sunset-flush'd: and, dew'd with show'ry drops,
Up-clomb the shadowy pine above the woven copse.

The charmed sunset linger'd low adown
In the red West: thro' mountain clefts the dale
Was seen far inland, and the yellow down
Border'd with palm, and many a winding vale
And meadow, set with slender galingale;
A land where all things always seem'd the same!
And round about the keel with faces pale,
Dark faces pale against that rosy flame,
The mild-eyed melancholy Lotos-eaters came.

Branches they bore of that enchanted stem,
Laden with flow'r and fruit, whereof they gave
To each, but whoso did receive of them,
And taste, to him the gushing of the wave
Far far away did seem to mourn and rave
On alien shores: and if his fellow spake,
His voice was thin, as voices from the grave:
And deep-asleep he seem'd, yet all awake,
And music in his ears his beating heart did make.

ἀργηστὴν ποταμὸν, μυχόθεν πελάγοσδε ῥέοντα,
θαύμασαν· ἀρχαίας δὲ νιφὸς κορυφὰς τρικαρήνους
ἄψοφα τηλεφανεῖ ῥόδεος βάλεν ἕσπερος αὐγῇ·
ἐν δὲ πίτυς πλεκτὴν δροσόεσσ' ἀνέτελλε καθ' ὕλην.

ἥλιος, ἀκροτάτοις ξανθῆς ἐπὶ τέρμασι γαίας,
παύετο δυόμενος, αἰὲν μέλλοντι ἐοικώς·[1]
πόῤῥω πουλύγναμπτα διὰ πτύχας ἔπρεπ' ὀρεινὰς
ἄγκεα καὶ βῆσσαι καὶ λειμῶνες κροκόβαπτοι,
φοινίκων τε περιστεφέες ῥαδίνων τε κυπείρων·
φάσμ' ἀστεμφὲς ἀεί· περὶ δὲ στειρὴν κατὰ κῦμα,
ὠχρὸν ἰδεῖν, φλόγεόν τε μελάγχρωτες παρὰ φέγγος,
ἠγερέθοντ', ἀγανοῖσι κατηφέες ὀφθαλμοῖσι,
Λωτοφάγοι.

τοὶ δὴ κλῶνας φέρον ἀνθεμοέντας,
καρποφόρον γάνος ἄῤῥητον, καὶ δῶκαν ἑκάστῳ·
οἱ δ' ἐπάσαντ', ἀμέτρητον ὑπεὶρ ἅλα κυματοαγῆ
ἄξεινον παρὰ θῖνα μινυρόμενον βακχεύειν
οἶδμ' ἐδόκει βομβῆεν· ἀραιὴ δ' ἵκετο φωνὴ[2]
φθεγγομένων, ὥς τις νεκύων ἀμένηνος ἀφ' Ἀΐδου·
ὕπνος ἔχειν ἀΰπνους, κραδίης τε παλίῤῥοθος ὁρμὴ
ἡδύ τι μελπομένῳ ἰνδάλλετο.

[1] *Od.* IX. 607. [2] Theocr. XIII. 59.

They sat them down upon the yellow sand,
Between the sun and moon upon the shore;
And sweet it was to dream of Fatherland,
Of child, and wife, and slave; but evermore
Most weary seem'd the sea, weary the oar,
Weary the wand'ring fields of barren foam.
Then some one said, "We will return no more:"
And all at once they sang, "Our island home
Is far beyond the wave: we will no longer roam."

CHORIC SONG.

There is sweet music here that softer falls
Than petals from blown roses on the grass,
Or night-dews on still waters between walls
Of shadowy granite, in a gleaming pass:
Music that gentlier on the spirit lies
Than tired eyelids upon tired eyes:
Music that brings sweet sleep down from the blissful skies.
Here are cool mosses deep,
And thro' the moss the ivies creep,
And in the stream the long-leav'd flowers weep,
And from the craggy ledge the poppy hangs in sleep.

οἱ δ' ἐκάθηντο,
μεσσηγὺς Φοίβου τε φάους δίας τε Σελήνης,
ξουθοῦ ἐπ' αἰγιαλοῦ· πέρι τ' ἄσμενοι ἐμνήσαντο
πατρίδα καὶ δμῶας, φίλα τέκνα, φίλας τε γυναῖκας·
κῦμα δὲ δυσφόρεον, καὶ ναυστολίην ἀλεγεινὴν,
καὶ πελάγη[1] ἀφροῖο πολυπλανῆ ἀτρυγέτοιο.
ὧδε δέ τις εἴπεσκεν, "Ἅλις πεπλανήμεθ', ἑταῖροι·"
αὐτίκ' ἄρα ξύμπαντες, "Ἀλίβροχον ἡμέτερον δῶ
εὖ μάλα μακρὸν ἄπεστιν, ἑκὰς ἐνὶ οἴνοπι πόντῳ
ὧδε μένειν ὄχ' ἄριστον· ἅλις πεπλανήμεθ', ἑταῖροι."

[2]ἅδιον μέλος ἐνθάδ', ἤ τις στρ.
ῥιπὰ πετάλου, ῥόδων ἐν ἀκμᾷ,
πόαν ἧκα βαλόντος· ἢ
νυκτιλαμπὲς ὑπόσκιον
ῥαίνουσα ψακὰς ἠρεμαῖον
κρύπτ' ἐνδόμυχον νᾶμ'·
οὐ τόσσον καμάτῳ φιλύπνους
γλήνας κατέθελξεν
κοῦφον ἐπὶ βλεφάρων βάρος ἐμπεσόν·
ἀκηδέων ἀφ' ἑδρᾶν
ἐπῳδαῖς μετεπέμψαθ' ὕπνον.
πάντη δ' ἐνὶ τάκεται[3] ῥεέθροις
ναρὸν τανύφυλλον ἔρνος·
βαθύστρωτον ἅδην διέρπει . ἀντιστρ.
ψυχρὰν στιβάδ' ἀμφὶ κισσός· εὕδει
προβλήτων σπιλάδων ἄπο
μάκων σῖγα καθημμένος.[4]

[1] *Od.* v. 335.
[2] Soph. *Œd. Col.* 668—719 (Dindorf. *Poetæ Scenici Græci.*)
[3] *Od.* VIII. 522. [4] Soph. *Antig.* 1222.

Why are we weigh'd upon with heaviness,
And utterly consum'd with sharp distress,
While all things else have rest from weariness?
All things have rest: why should we toil alone,
We only toil, who are the first of things,
And make perpetual moan,
Still from one sorrow to another thrown:
Nor ever fold our wings,
And cease from wanderings:
Nor steep our brows in slumber's holy balm;
Nor hearken what the inner spirit sings,
"There is no joy but calm!"
Why should we only toil, the roof and crown of things?

Lo! in the middle of the wood
The folded leaf is woo'd from out the bud
With winds upon the branch, and there
Grows green and broad, and takes no care,
Sun-steep'd at noon, and in the moon
Nightly dew-fed: and turning yellow
Falls, and floats adown the air.

αἴ, αἴ, θυμοβόροις πονοῦμεν
ταλαίφρονες αὔτως
ἀνακεστοτάταις ἀνίαις
ἡμεῖς· πάρα δ' ἄλλοις
δῖα λυγρᾶς ἀνάπαυσις ὀϊζύος,
ὅσ' ἔστιν· ἦ μόνοισιν
εἵμαρται καμάτων ἀφύκτων
στένειν ἀλίαστα, θεῶν μετ' ἔργοις
πρωτεῖα μάταν λαχοῦσιν;
ἡμῖν τοῖς ὑπεράλλοις, χθονίων τοῖς μεγ' ἀρίστοις, στρ.
ὄρνις ὣς πτερύγων ἀκάματός τις πολυπλάγκτοισιν ἐρετμοῖς,[1]
ὕπνοιο κηληθμὸς ἀμβρότοιο
ἆρ' οὔποτ' ἐμβάψει κάρα;
πόνων ἄγευστος λέλογχεν ὄλβον,
ἔναυλον τόδ' ἐφυμνεῖ 'ν φρεσὶ δαίμων.

φεῦ· ὕλας ἐν ὀμφαλοῖσιν ἀβρότοισι,
βλάσταν φύλλον ὑπεκδὺν, ἀνέμου σαινόμενον κιναθίσμασι,
χλωρὸν εὐρυφυὲς βρύει,
ἀκτῖνες δ' ἀμέριμνον
ἔνδιον, νυχίᾳ δ' αὖτε σελάνα τρέφεν ἔρσᾳ· ἀντ.
τέλος δ' ἀλλόχροον ῥεῖ, κατὰ δ' οὖρον μετέωρον διαφεύγει.

[1] Æsch. *Agam.* 52.

Lo! sweeten'd with the summer light,
The full-juic'd apple, waxing over-mellow,
Drops in a silent autumn night.
All its allotted length of days,
The flower ripens in its place,
Ripens and fades, and falls, and hath no toil,
Fast-rooted in the fruitful soil.

Hateful is the dark-blue sky
Vaulted o'er the dark-blue sea.
Death is the end of life: ah, why
Should life all labour be?
Let us alone. Time driveth onward fast,
And in a little while our lips are dumb.
Let us alone. What is it that will last?
All things are taken from us, and become
Portions and parcels of the dreadful Past.
Let us alone. What pleasure can we have
To war with evil? Is there any peace
In ever climbing up the climbing wave?
All things have rest, and ripen tow'rd the grave
In silence; ripen, fall and cease.
Give us long rest or death, dark death, or dreamful ease!

θέρους ἐν αὐγαῖς πέπον τεθηλὸς,
ὡραῖον ἔπεσεν ἔννυχον
ἄκρας ὀπώρας ἄφωνα μᾶλον.
ζωᾶς μοιρίδιον τέρμα τελείας
ἀνθέων γένη κατάνυσ' ἀδυόσμων,
ἀκμάζοντ' ἀπόνως, φροῦδα δ' ἔπειτ' ᾤχετ' ἐπασσυτέρᾳ ῥοπᾷ,
εὐκάρποισι δυσεκλύτως
ἐῤῥιζωμέν' ἀρούραις.

[1] στυγνὸν πόλου κυάνεον στρ.
βάθος πάλαι πορφυροειδοῦς
ὑπερτέταται θαλάττας·
ζῶσιν θάνατος πέπρωται·
ζῶντες δ' ἀπαύστῳ πόνῳ ἄλλως βίον ἀντλοῦμεν·
ἐᾶτ'· ἐσσυμένων ῥίμφ' ἐνιαύτων
σιγᾷ τάχ' ἔπεισιν· οὔδεν
σταθμὸν ἔχει βέβαιον.
πάντ' ἐκλέλοιπεν, φοβερῷ ἀντιστρ.
δὲ τῶν πάλαι σύζυγ' ὁμίλῳ
φεύγει· τί δ' ἀτερπὲς αἰὲν
ἀδμῆτ', ἀμάχου κατ' ἄτας,
κλύδων' ἔπ' ἀμβαίνομεν; ἔσθ' ἀσυχίας πᾶσιν
σὺγ' εἰσερχομένας μοῖρα καθ ὥραν·
τᾶς πουλυπλάνων ὀνείρων,
ἤ θανάτου τύχοιμεν.

[1] Soph. *Antig.* 781—800.

How sweet it were, hearing the downward stream,
With half-shut eyes ever to seem
Falling asleep in a half-dream!
To dream and dream, like yonder amber light,
Which will not leave the myrrh-bush on the height;
To hear each other's whisper'd speech;
Eating the Lotos, day by day,
To watch the crisping ripples on the beach,
And tender curving lines of creamy spray:
To lend our hearts and spirits wholly
To the influence of mild-minded melancholy;
To muse and brood and live again in memory,
With those old faces of our infancy
Heap'd over with a mound of grass,
Two handfuls of white dust, shut in an urn of brass!

Dear is the mem'ry of our wedded lives,
And dear the last embraces of our wives
And their warm tears; but all hath suffer'd change:
For surely now our household hearths are cold:
Our sons inherit us: our looks are strange:

[1] ἢ τερπνὸν μάλα, παγῶν   στρ.
πὰρ κλινθέντα καταῤῥόοισιν,
ἀεὶ βλεφάροις ὑπνῶδες ἡμι-
κλείστοις ὧδ' ὅσον οὐ καθεύδειν·
ἠλεκτροφαῆ κατ' αὐγὰν
ὑψοῦ 'πὶ μυῤῥίνου
βάτου μόνιμον· καθ' ἁμέ-
ραν ψιθυρὸν ἀντιφωνεῖν,
κυμάτι' αἰγιαλῷ
κυρτωθένθ' ἁπαλὰ σκοπεῖν, γαλακτώ-
δη τ' ἀφρὸν πολύκυκλον·   ἀντιστρ.
σὲ, δέσποιν' ἀγάνοφρον, αἰνεῖν,
τὰν Λωτοφάγοις φίλαν, Κατηφεί-
α· βυσσόφρονι πολλὰ θυμῷ
εἴδωλα πάλαι θανόντων,
οἷσιν βρέφη σύνη-
μεν, νῦν σποδὸν ἐξίτηλον
χαλκέλατον ἄγγος ἔνδον
χώμασι τυμβοχόοις
εἴργει, φαντασίαις πάλιν προσαυδᾶν.

[2] ἀδύ τι κουριδίων ἐνθυμεῖσθαι ὑμεναίων·   στρ.
φίλαι χερῶν περιπτυχαὶ,
καὶ δακρύων μνάμα· τὰ δὲ πανταχοῦ ἠλλοίωται·
ἡμῶν γὰρ ἐφέστιον οὖδας
κλαρονόμον κατέχει γένος, ἢ ξένων

[1] Eur. *Hecub.* 444—465.   [2] Soph. *Œd. Tyr.* 151—166.

And we should come like ghosts to trouble joy:
Or else the island-princes over-bold
Have eat our substance, and the minstrel sings
Before them of the ten-years' war in Troy,
And our great deeds, as half forgotten things.
Is there confusion in the little isle?
Let what is broken so remain.
The Gods are hard to reconcile:
'Tis hard to settle order once again.
There *is* confusion worse than death,
Trouble on trouble, pain on pain,
Long labour unto aged breath,
Sore task to hearts worn out with many wars,
And eyes grown dim with gazing on the pilot-stars.

But, propt on beds of amaranth and moly,
How sweet, while warm airs lull us, breathing lowly,
With half-dropt eyelids still,
Beneath a heaven dark and holy,
To watch the long bright river drawing slowly
His waters from the purple hill—
To hear the dewy echoes calling
From cave to cave thro' the thick-twined vine—

ἐς ὑπερηνορίᾳ· παρὰ δ' ἄμναστον πολέμου λόγον
  ἔργα τ' ἀριστήων, θεῖός τις ἀοιδὸς ἐφυμνεῖ·
ἡμεῖς λυγρὸν ἰδεῖν, ὥς τις παλίνορσος ἀφ' Αΐδου. ἀντ.
    τὰ δ' ἐῤῥέτω δυσέξοδα,
Θεοὶ μάλ' ἀμείλικτοι, νάσῳ δ' ἔνι κόσμος ἄκοσμος·
    ἔστιν θανάτου τι χέρειον,
  ἄλγος ἐπ' ἄλγεσι γῆρας ἐπ' ἔσχατον,
ἢ θυμῷ κακὸν ἄχθος ἅδην πολέμοις κεκορημένῳ,
ὄμμασί τ' ἀμβλυνθεῖσι πρὸς ἄστροισιν φιλοναύταις.[1]

[2]μῶλυ κάτ', εἶτ' ἀμαραν- στρ.
τίναν στιβάδ' εὔστρωτον,
  ὑπνώσσουσι βλεφάροις,
  λεπτὰ Ζεφύρων πνεόντων,
  ὑπό τ' οὐρανοῦ κνέφας
  ἀμβροσίου, δολιχὰς
    ποταμίας ὁρᾷν
ἧκα ῥεούσας ἀπὸ πορφυρωδῶν
  βούνων ὑπὲκ προχοάς· τὰ δ' Ἀχοῦς
  κελεύσμαθ' ὑγρᾶς ἐπάλληλα
  σπέσσιν ἐν ἀντιτύποις ἀντιστρ.
  ὕλαν διὰ καλλίβοτρυν,

[1] Scott-Liddell *Lex. in voc.* [2] Eur. *Hippol.* 121—140.

To hear the em'rald-colour'd water falling
Thro' many a wov'n acanthus-wreath divine!
Only to hear and see the far-off sparkling brine,
Only to hear were sweet, stretch'd out beneath the pine.

The Lotos blooms below the flow'ry peak:
The Lotos blows by every winding creek:
All day the wind breathes low with mellower tone:
Thro' ev'ry hollow cave and alley lone
Round and round the spicy downs the Yellow Lotos-dust is blown.
We have had enough of action, and of motion we,
Roll'd to starboard, roll'd to larboard, when the surge was seething free,
Where the wallowing monster spouted his foam-fountains in the sea.
Let us swear an oath, and keep it with an equal mind,
In the hollow Lotos-land to live and lie reclin'd
On the hills like Gods together, careless of mankind:

ἤ που κυάνεον ὧδ'
ὕδωρ μετ' ἀκανθίνοισι
πολυδαιδάλοις πλοκαῖς
θεσπεσίοις κελάρυ-
ζον, ἀπόνως κλύειν·
πόῤῥωθεν ἅλμαν ἐσιδεῖν φαεννὰν,
ὕψαυχεν' εἴθ' ὑπὸ δένδρ' ἀκούειν·
τούτοις βίον ἔστι ποιμαίνειν.

παρά τ' εὐανθῶν κορυφὰς πρώνων
πορθμῶν τ' ἐσόδους αἰολομόρφων
λώτου θαλερὸν γάνος ἀκμάζει·
πνεῖ παννῆμαρ μαλθακὸς ἀήρ·
κοῖλα κατ' ἄντρα καὶ οἰόπολ' ἄγκη,
περὶ λειμώνων πλάτος εὐόσμων,
ξανθοῦ σπέρματα
λώτου φέρεται πολυδινῆ.
ἅλις εἴργασται καὶ πεπόνηται
νῦν ἐπὶ δεξιὰ νῦν ἐπ' ἀριστερὰ
λαβρῷ κύματι ποντοτινάκτοις,
ἔνθα πελώριον ὕψόσ' ἐφύσα
προκυλινδόμενον κῆτος ἀφρώδους
οἴδματος ἄχναν.
ἀγετ' οὖν ὀχυραῖς ὅρκια βουλαῖς
θῶμεν, σύμφονες ὧδε διαζῆν,
τρόπον ἀθανάτων, οἵτ' ἐν Ὀλύμπῳ
παρὰ νεκταρέοις κεῖνται πώμασιν
εἰκῆ χθονίων ἀμελοῦντες·

For they lie beside their nectar, and the bolts are hurl'd
Far below them in the valleys, and the clouds are lightly curl'd
Round their golden houses, girdled with the gleaming world:
Where they smile in secret, looking over wasted lands,
Blight and famine, plague and earthquake, roaring deeps and fiery sands,
Clanging fights, and flaming towns, and sinking ships, and praying hands.
But they smile, they find a music centred in a doleful song,
Steaming up, a lamentation and an ancient tale of wrong,
Like a tale of little meaning though the words are strong;
Chanted from an ill-us'd race of men that cleave the soil,
Sow the seed, and reap the harvest with enduring toil,
Storing yearly little dues of wheat, and wine, and oil:

τῆλε δ' ἐν οὔρεσι βροντὰ καναχεῖ
χρύσεα δώματα πρὸς θεοτερπῆ,
στροφοδινοῦνταί τ' ἀμφὶς νεφελαί,
περὶ δ' οὐράνιος
στίλβει πόλος ἀστεροφεγγής.
οἱ δ' ὀρυμάγδῳ γᾶν βροτολοίγῳ
διαπερθομέναν, βρύχιον πέλαγος,
χθόνα σεισθεῖσαν, ψάμμον φλογέαν,
ὀλοᾷ λοιμοῦ λιμὸν ἐπ' ἄτῃ,
καταθραυομένας ναῦς ἐνὶ κύμασιν,
ἀστέων ἄμοτον πῦρ καιομένων,
χεῖράς θ' ἱκετῶν,
λάθρα χαίρουσιν ὁρῶντες·
τὸ δὲ θρηνῶδες μέλος ὠγύγιον
πέρι τερπομένοις ὦσι δέχονται,
κοὐκ ἀλέγουσιν δεινὰ λεγόντων,
τὸ παρ' ἀνθρώπων αἰκιζομένων
εἰσαναβαῖνον δώματ' Ὀλύμπου·
τῶν τλασιπόνων, τῶν ἀροτήρων,
φιτυθείσας οἵ τ' ἀπὸ γαίας
σῖτον ἐτήσιον, οἶνον, ἔλαιον,
διασώζουσιν κομίσαντες.

Till they perish, and they suffer—some, 'tis whisper'd—down in hell
Suffer endless anguish, others in Elysian valleys dwell,
Resting weary limbs at length on beds of asphodel.
Surely, surely, slumber is more sweet than toil, the shore
Than labour in mid-ocean, wind and wave, and oar;
Oh rest ye, brother-mariners, we will not wander more.

θανατωθέντες δ' οἱ μὲν ἐν Αΐδου,
τοιάδε φάμα θρυλεῖ ψιθυρὰ,
διακναιόμενοι πῆμ' ἀθλεύουσ',[1]
οἱ δ' ἐνὶ βάσσαις 'Ηλυσιαῖσιν,
καμάτων ἐσαεὶ γυῖα λυθέντες,
κατά τ' ἀσφοδέλου
δέμνι' ἄλυποι διάγουσιν.
ἔστ' ἀναπαύλας, ἔστ' ἐπὶ χερσοῦ
γέρας ἅδιον, τοῦτο σαφέστατον,
ἠὲ βαθύπλοον, ἠὲ δυσάνεμον
αἰὲν ἐρετμοῦ κόπον ἐξαντλεῖν.
λήγετε μόχθων,
φεῦ μόχθων λήγεθ', ἑταῖροι.

L. 1860.

[1] Æsch. *Prom.* 94.

From Milton's Comus.

I had not thought to have unlock'd my lips
In this unhallow'd air, but that this juggler
Would think to charm my judgment, as mine eyes,
Obtruding false rules prank'd in reason's garb.
I hate when Vice can bolt her arguments,
And Virtue has no tongue to check her pride.—
Impostor! do not charge most innocent Nature.
As if she would her children should be riotous
With her abundance; she, good cateress,
Means her provision only to the good,
That live according to her sober laws,
And holy dictate of spare Temperance:
If every just man, that now pines with want,
Had but a moderate and beseeming share
Of that which lewdly pamper'd Luxury
Now heaps upon some few with vast excess,
Nature's full blessings would be well dispensed
In unsuperfluous even proportion,
And she no wit encumber'd with her store;
And then the Giver would be better thank'd,
His praise due paid: for swinish Gluttony
Ne'er looks to Heaven amidst his gorgeous feast,
But with besotted base ingratitude
Crams, and blasphemes his Feeder. Shall I go on?

'Ουχ εἰλόμην ἂν, οὐ, καταπτύστῳ 'ν τόπῳ
εἰ μὴ τὸ σιγᾶν· ὁ δὲ γοητείᾳ φρένας,
τῶν ὀμμάτων γὰρ οὐ μέλει, παρεκτρέπειν
ἔμελλ' ἀλαζὼν, ξυμπλάσας εὐσχημόνως
τὸ ψεῦδος· ἔχθιστον δέ μοι πάντων τόδε,
λαλεῖν τὸ φαῦλον, τἀγαθὸν φώνην στέγειν.
μή μοι, δολοφρὸν, τὴν Φύσιν, κεδνὴν θεὰν,
τλήσῃς ἀσελγῶν, οἷς τὰ δῶρ' ἀπώλεσε
διαστρέφων τις, αἰτιάσασθαι τρόπων·
ἥτις μόνοισι τοῖσι σωφρόνων νόμων
τῆς ἐγκρατείας εὐσεβῶν θ' ὑπηκόοις,
καλῶς προβουλεύουσα, πορσύνει τροφήν.
εἴθ' ὤφελεν γὰρ πᾶς τις, ὃς πτωχὸς στένει
δίκαια τηρῶν, ὧν ὑπέρκοπος χλιδὴ
παύροις ἐπεγχεῖ, μετρίας μοίρας τυχεῖν·
ὡς ἦν ἂν εὐάρμοστα τοῦ θεοῦ γέρα
λαχεῖν ἕκαστον, διανεμόντος ἀφθόνως.
ὁ δ' αὖ λατρείας τῆς προσηκούσης τότε
οὐχ, ὡς τανῦν, ἥμαρτ' ἄν. οὐ γὰρ ἔσθ' ὅπως
θοιναῖσι γαστρίμαργος ἀπλήστοις ἔνι
θεοῦ φροντιεῖ τις τοῦ τὸ πᾶν δεδωκότος·
ἀλλ' αἰσχροποιὸς καὶ φρενῶν κεκομμένος
δείπνοις ἐν αὐτοῖς τὸν πορόντα λοιδορεῖ.

Or have I said enough? To him that dares
Arm his profane tongue with contemptuous words
Against the sun-clad Power of Chastity,
Fain would I something say, yet to what end?
Thou hast nor ear nor soul to apprehend
The sublime notion and high mystery,
Thus must be utter'd to unfold the sage
And serious doctrine of Virginity;
And thou art worthy that thou shouldst not know
More happiness than this thy present lot.
Enjoy your dear wit and gay rhetoric,
That hath so well been taught her dazzling fence;
Thou art not fit to hear thyself convinced:
Yet, should I try, the uncontrolled worth
Of this pure cause would kindle my rapt spirits
To such a flame of sacred vehemence,
That dumb things would be moved to sympathize,
And the brute Earth would lend her nerves, and shake,
Till all thy magic structures, rear'd so high,
Were shatter'd into heaps o'er thy false head.

τάδ' οὖν λελέχθω· καίπερ ὃς τὸ πάρθενον
ἔτλη, τὸ θεῖον ἠμφιεσμένον σέλας,
γλώσσης βεβήλου κερτόμοις ὀνείδεσι
βαλεῖν ἀναιδὴς, ἀσμένη πρὸς τοῦτον ἂν
μῦθόν τιν' ἐντείναιμ' ἄπρακτος οὖσ' ὅμως.
σὲ γὰρ, τὸν ἄψυχόν τε καὶ κωφὸν, λέγω,
τὸν οὐκ ἔχοντα τὴν ἀνυμφεύτῳ βίῳ
σοφίαν ἐνοῦσαν εἰσιδεῖν, πολλοῦ γε δεῖ·
σεμν' ἔστι ταῦτ', οὐδ' ἔστιν ἀμυήτοις μαθεῖν
θεσμῶν κρυφαίους ὑψιγεννήτων λόγους.
στέρξον φυλάσσων ἃ 'λαβες· τοῖος γὰρ εἶ.
ὄναιο δῆτα τῆς φίλης γλωσσαλγίας,
καὶ κομψότητος λογομάχων σοφισμάτων·
οὐδ' ὣς ἐλεγχθησόμενος· οὐ γὰρ ἄξιος.
εἰ δ' ἤθελόν ποθ', ἥδ' ἐμὴ πυριφλεγεῖ
ἀγῶνος ὀτρυνθεῖσα τηλικοῦ μένει
φρὴν εἰς τόσονδε σφοδρότητος ἦλθεν ἂν
θεοσσύτοις ὁρμαῖσιν, ὥστ' αἴνου τυχεῖν
κᾀκ τῶν ἀφώνων, παράνομον κινουμένων·
κᾀμοὶ ξύνεργος γαῖ', ἀναίσθητος τὸ πρὶν,
ταῦθ' ὑψίπυργα σῆς χερὸς φαντάσματ' ἂν
σοὶ δὴ σαλευθεῖσ' ἐγκατέσκηψεν, φέναξ,
καταῤῥαγέντα καὶ διεσκεδασμένα. L. 1862.

Ode to Adversity.

DAUGHTER of Jove, relentless power,
Thou tamer of the human breast,
Whose iron scourge and torturing hour,
The bad affright, afflict the best!
Bound in thy adamantine chain,
The proud are taught to taste of pain,
And purple tyrants vainly groan
With pangs unfelt before, unpitied and alone.

When first thy Sire to send on earth
Virtue, his darling child, design'd,
To thee he gave the heav'nly birth,
And bade to form her infant mind.
Stern rugged Nurse! thy rigid lore
With patience many a year she bore;
What sorrow was, thou bad'st her know,
And from her own she learn'd to melt at others' woe.

GRAY.

Quæ sævo domitos imperio regis
Mortales, superi nata Jovis Dea,
  Dira non sine pœna et
    Flagris improba ferreis

Pertentans homines; unde adamantinis
Sub vinclis trepidum comprimitur Nefas,
  Anguntur que malorum
    Seris pectora luctibus,

Nec puri sceleris non animi dolent;
Te reges dominam purpurei novam,
  Per deserta domorum,
    Te vano gemitu tremunt.

Cum lectam generi mittere filiam
Humano voluit cœlicolum Pater
  Virtutem, tibi diam
    Commisit sobolem Deus,

Ut prudens teneræ pectora fingeres:
Ah! quanta rigidam te patientia,
  Nutrix aspera, longis
    Virtus temporibus tulit!

Sensit, qua miseris fracta doloribus
Mens cura gemeret: sensit, et haud suo,
  Te perdocta magistra,
    Luctu tangitur invicem.

L. 1837.

The Deserted Village.

How often have I paused on every charm,
The sheltered cot and cultivated farm,
The never-failing brook and busy mill,
The decent church that topt the neighbouring hill,
The hawthorn bush, with seats beneath the shade,
For talking age and whispering lovers made!
How often have I blest the coming day,
When toil remitting lent its turn to play,
And all the village train, from labour free,
Led up their sports beneath the spreading tree;
While many a pastime circled in the shade,
The young contending, as the old surveyed;
And many a gambol frolicked o'er the ground,
And sleights of art and feats of strength went round;
And still as each repeated pleasure tired,
Succeeding sports the mirthful band inspired:
The dancing pair that simply sought renown
By holding out to tire each other down;
The swain mistrustless of his smutted face,
While secret laughter tittered round the place;
The bashful virgin's sidelong looks of love,
The matron's glance that would these looks reprove—
These were thy charms, sweet Village; sports like these
With sweet succession taught even toil to please;
These round thy bowers their cheerful influence shed:
These were thy charms—but all these charms are fled.

GOLDSMITH.

Ah! quoties illo cessabam lentus in agro,
Miratus placidas culta per arva casas,
Et loca qua pistrina sequacibus adstrepit undis,
Mundaque vicinis addita templa jugis,
Et frutices lætos, aptasque sedentibus umbras,
Seu senium musset, sive susurret amor.
Ah! quoties grato venerabar pectore lucem,
Cum misso exciperent pensa labore joci,
Multaque ruricolæ properarent agmina turbæ
Ducere sub patula fronde soluta choros.
Tum fuit umbrosa quantum certamen arena!
Colludunt juvenes, aspiciuntque senes;
Innumerosque cient vexato in gramine gyros,
Membrorum vegeta vi, celerique manu.
Displiceat toties eadem repetita voluptas?
Inveniet ludos læta caterva novos.
Certatim innocuam qui produxere choream,
Saltando ut facilis gloria parta foret;
Rusticus inspersa fœdus fuligine vultum,
Qui movet occultos, nescius ipse, jocos;
Virginis indictam prodentia lumina flammam,
Quæque oculo mater vix prohibere velit—
Hos comites inter, sedes dilecta, laboris
Dulcibus immisti lene placebat onus;
Hæc tibi tranquillam spirabant undique pacem;
Hæc tibi—sed notos deseruere locos!

L. 1838.

Oenone.

THERE is a vale in Ida, lovelier
Than all the valleys of Ionian hills.
The swimming vapour slopes athwart the glen,
Puts forth an arm, and creeps from pine to pine,
And loiters, slowly drawn. On either hand
The lawns and meadow-ledges midway down
Hang rich in flowers, and far below them roars
The long brook falling thro' the clov'n ravine
In cataract after cataract to the sea.
Behind the valley, topmost Gargarus
Stands up and takes the morning; but in front
The gorges, opening wide apart, reveal
Troas and Ilion's column'd citadel,
The crown of Troas.

UT POTUIT
EXIMIUM HOC CARMEN
IN AMŒNIS
APUD FALCONHURST OTIIS
LATINE REDDIDIT
ET
JOANNI G. TALBOT
OPTIMO AMICISSIMO
DENIQUE GENERO
D. D.
L.

Est Ida in media vallis, quot Ionia valles
Alma fovet, forma superans. Ibi saltibus hærent
Et lenti flultant inter pineta vapores.
At gravidos multis decorant pendentia prata
Floribus hinc illinc montes : rivusque reductas
Desilit in rupes, reboatque anfractibus imis,
Oceani longinqua petens. Hîc Gargarus ingens
Praeripit Auroram : sed ab illa parte, revulsis
Faucibus, apparet celsis speciosa columnis
Troas, et Iliacæ, decus illæ Troadis, arces.

Hither came at noon
Mournful Œnone, wandering forlorn
Of Paris, once her playmate on the hills.
Her cheek had lost the rose, and round her neck
Floated her hair, or seem'd to float, in rest.
She, leaning on a fragment twined with vine,
Sang to the stillness, till the mountain shade
Sloped downward to her seat from the upper cliff.

"O mother Ida, many-fountain'd Ida,
Dear mother Ida, hearken ere I die!
For now the noonday quiet holds the hill:
The grasshopper is silent in the grass:
The lizard, with her shadow on the stone,
Rests like a shadow; and the cicala sleeps.
The purple flowers droop: the golden bee
Is lily-cradled: I alone awake.
My eyes are full of tears, my heart of love;
My heart is breaking, and my eyes are dim,
And I am all a-weary of my life.

"O mother Ida, many-fountain'd Ida,
Dear mother Ida, hearken ere I die!
Hear me, O earth! hear me O hills! O caves

Huc adiit, rapido medii sub sole diei,
Solivaga Œnone, Paridem fletura sodalem.
At tenera in cervice comæ jacuere solutæ:
Nec roseæ fulsere genæ. Sub rupe reclinis
Vitibus intexta, longo tranquilla locorum
Carmine mulcebat, donec demissa sedentem
Velavit summis paulatim à montibus umbra.

"Me miseram exaudi scatebroso à culmine, mater!
Ida meam, genitrix, mors advenit, accipe vocem.
Jam colles siluere; silent per prata locustæ:
Glauca lacerta jacens, in saxum projicit umbram,
Ipsa umbram referens. Inter cunabula florum
Aurea dormit apis: dormit tranquilla cicada:
Languent purpurei flores. Ego sola soporis
Inscia: me flentes oculi, me cordis amores,
Me luctus, duræque tenent mala tædia vitæ.

"Me miseram exaudi scatebroso à culmine, mater!
Ida meam, genitrix, mors advenit, accipe vocem.
Proh juga, proh tellus, gelidisque audite cavernæ

That house the cold crown'd snake! O mountain brooks,
I am the daughter of a river-god;
Hear me, for I will speak, and build up all
My sorrow with my song, as yonder walls
Rose slowly to a music slowly breathed,
A cloud that gather'd shape: for it may be
That while I speak of it, a little while
My heart may wander from its deeper woe.

"O mother Ida, many-fountain'd Ida,
Dear mother Ida, hearken ere I die!
I waited underneath the dawning hills,
Aloft the mountain lawn was dewy-dark,
And dewy-dark aloft the mountain pine:
Beautiful Paris, evil-hearted Paris,
Leading a jet-black goat, white-horn'd, white-hoof'd,
Came up from reedy Simois all alone.

"O mother Ida, hearken ere I die!
Far off the torrent called me from the cleft:
Far up the solitary morning smote
The streaks of virgin snow. With down-dropt eyes

Anguibus implicitæ, celeresque è montibus amnes!
Me Numen genuit fluviale. Ego, qualia lentum
Lente illa ad cantum, (nubi velut indita forma,)
Mœnia surrexisse ferunt, ita carmine luctum
Informare velim, soliti si forte doloris
Infixum liceat tantillum fallere vulnus.

"Me miseram exaudi scatebroso à culmine, mater!
Ida meam, genitrix, mors advenit, accipe vocem.
Suspiciens montes incerta luce rubentes,
Et gelido pinus suffusas rore, sedebam:
Cum Paris, heu! nimium pulchri sub tegmine vultus
Turpia corda fovens, albis et cornibus hircum
Insignem pedibusque adducens, cætera nigrum,
Solus arundinea venit Simoentis ab unda.

"Ida meam, genitrix, mors advenit, accipe vocem.
At me præcipites procul e convallibus undæ
Visæ compellare: procul, super invia montis,
Incedens tacito signabat culmina gressu,
Et puras Aurora nives. Ego sola sedebam

I sat alone: white-breasted, like a star
Fronting the dawn, he moved: a leopard-skin
Droop'd from his shoulder, but his sunny hair
Cluster'd about his temples like a god's;
And his cheek brighten'd, as the foambow brightens
When the wind blows the foam, and all my heart
Went forth to embrace him coming ere he came.

"Dear mother Ida, hearken ere I die!
He smiled, and opening out his milk-white palm
Disclosed a fruit of pure Hesperian gold,
That smelt ambrosially, and while I look'd
And listen'd, the full-flowing river of speech
Came down upon my heart. 'My own Œnone,
Beautiful-brow'd Œnone, my own soul,
Behold this fruit, whose gleaming rind, ingrav'n
"For the most fair," would seem to award it thine,
As lovelier than whatever Oread haunt
The knolls of Ida, loveliest in all grace
Of movement, and the charm of married brows.'

"Dear mother Ida, hearken ere I die!
He press'd the blossom of his lips to mine,
And added, 'This was cast upon the board,

Triste tuens: illum mox albo pectore, ut atras
Stella fugat penetrans adversa fronte tenebras,
Vidi affulgentem. Lateris gestamina pulchri
Exuviæ pardi pendebant, diaque flavis
Fluctibus undantes velabant tempora crines,
Splendebantque genæ, qualis, cum ventus aquosam
Fert agitans spumam, nitet arcus in ætheris auras.
Illum amplexa oculis, totoque e corde vocavi.

"Ida meam, genitrix, mors advenit, accipe vocem.
Continuo flavum, quod lactea dextra tenebat,
Ostendit malum, Hesperioque insignius auro,
Purique ambrosios exspirans roris odores,
Risitque alludens. Arrecta mente manebam:
Protinus è suavi manantia verba labello
Cor pepulere meum: 'Speciosam candida frontem,
Œnone, mea vita, hujusne in cortice pomi
Inscriptum, "Capiat quæ sit pulcherrima," cernis?
O quæ nec faciles motus, neque frontis amœnam
Juncturam, Phrygiæ decedis Oreasin Idæ,
Nonne tibi meritam liceat captare coronam?'

"Ida meam, genitrix, mors advenit, accipe vocem.
Labris labra meis, roseum referentia florem,
Admovit, dixitque: 'Vides, quod fertur amaras,

When all the full-faced presence of the gods
Ranged in the halls of Peleus: whereupon
Rose feud, with question unto whom 'twere due:
But lightfoot Iris brought it yester-eve,
Delivering that to me, by common voice
Elected umpire, Here comes to-day,
Pallas and Aphrodite, claiming each
This meed of fairest. Thou, within the cave
Behind yon whispering tuft of oldest pine,
May'st well behold them unbeheld, unheard
Hear all, and see thy Paris judge of gods.'

"Dear mother Ida, hearken ere I die!
It was the deep midnoon: one silvery cloud
Had lost his way between the piney sides
Of this lone glen. Then to the bower they came;
Naked they came to that smooth-swarded bower,
And at their feet the crocus brake like fire,
Violet, amaracus, and asphodel,
Lotos, and lilies: and a wind arose,
And overhead the wandering ivy and vine,
This way and that, in many a wild festoon
Ran riot, garlanding the gnarled boughs
With bunch and berry and flower thro' and thro'.

Dîs amplo aspectu Pelei celebrantibus aulam,
Appositum rixas genuisse. Hoc nuntia malum
Detulit en! Iris celeri velocior aura,
Et mihi permissum communi fœdere palmæ
Tradidit arbitrium. Quin mox cum Pallade Juno
Concurrens aderit magna ad certamina formæ,
Et Cytherea Venus. Tu, qua longæva susurrant
Pineta, antrorum videas celata latebris
Me Paridem tantas Superum componere lites.'

"Ida meam, genitrix, mors advenit, accipe vocem.
Arduus in medio flagrabat Phœbus Olympo:
Unaque, protenti latera inter pinea saltus,
Errabat nubes. Herbosum adeuntibus antrum,
Fulgida, sub pedibus nudarum, copia florum,
Lilia cum violis et amaracus asphodelusque
Ludere, cum loto, vitesque hederæque vagantes
Desuper innumeras vento intertexere vittas,
Mistaque baccarum in vario cum flore racemo
Infula nodosis frondes involvere ramis.

"O mother Ida, hearken ere I die!
On the tree-tops a crested peacock lit,
And o'er him flow'd a golden cloud, and lean'd
Upon him, slowly dropping fragrant dew.
Then first I heard the voice of her to whom,
Coming thro' heaven, like a light that grows
Larger and clearer, with one mind the gods
Rise up for reverence. She to Paris made
Proffer of royal power, ample rule
Unquestion'd, overflowing revenue
Wherewith to embellish state, 'From many a vale
And river-sunder'd champaign clothed with corn,
Or labour'd mines undrainable of ore.
Honour,' she said, 'and homage, tax and toll,
From many an inland town and haven large,
Mast-throng'd beneath her shadowing citadel,
In glassy bays among her tallest towers.'

"O mother Ida, hearken ere I die!
Still she spake on, and still she spake of power,
'Which in all action is the end of all;
Power fitted to the season; wisdom-bred
And throned of wisdom; from all neighbour crowns
Alliance and allegiance, till thy hand

"Ida, meam, genitrix, mors advenit, accipe vocem.
Tum super arboribus summis delapsa morari
Visa, et odoriferum sensim diffundere rorem
Aurea cristati nubes pavonis in alas.
Protinus audiri, cui per cœlestia regna
Grassanti, ut lumen majores crescit in orbes,
Unanimi assurgunt Superi. 'Tibi regis honores,
Intactæ ditionis opes, quascunque vel arva
Fluminis ad ripas interlabentis amœnas
Fertilia effundant, vel terra effossa metallis
Reddat inexhaustis, mea sunt donanda: vel urbes
Larga e congestis quæ vectigalia gazis
Contulerint, pelagique procul cogenda par undas
Qua vitreo in portus glomeratos æquore malos
Despiciunt veteres summis a turribus arces.'

"Ida meam, genitrix, mors advenit, accipe vocem.
'A me,' continuo, 'tibi derivata vigebit
Illa homini finis rerum, opportuna Potestas,
Cui nutrix propriam dederit Sapientia sedem:
Unde et finitimi, donec moritura resignet
Sceptra manus, reges sociata et subdita jungant

Fail from the sceptre-staff. Such boon from me,
From me, heav'n's queen, Paris, to thee king-born,
A shepherd all thy life, but yet king-born,
Should come most welcome, seeing men in power
Only are likest gods, who have attain'd
Rest in a happy place and quiet seats
Above the thunder, with undying bliss
In knowledge of their own supremacy.'

"Dear mother Ida, hearken ere I die!
She ceased: and Paris held the costly fruit
Out at arm's length, so much the thought of power
Flatter'd his spirit; but Pallas,—where she stood
Somewhat apart, her clear and bared limbs
O'erthwarted with the brazen-headed spear,
Upon her pearly shoulder leaning cold,
The while, above, her full and earnest eye
Over her snow-cold breast and angry cheek
Kept watch, waiting decision, made reply:
'Self-reverence, self-knowledge, self-control,
These three alone lead life to sovereign power.
Yet not for power (power of herself
Would come uncall'd for), but to live by law,
Acting the law we live by without fear;

Jura tuis. Tibi, pastor adhuc, sed regia proles,
Hæc, regina Deum, quæ sint gratissima, servo:
Non aliter Dis æquando, trans fulminis ortum
Æternam nactis propria inter regna quietem.'

"Ida meam, genitrix, mors advenit, accipe vocem.
Desiit: et Paridem, promisso munere lætum,
Vidi ego tendentum cum optato brachia pomo:
Sed Pallas, nudos semota ubi constitit artus
Effulgens, humerosque hasta trajecta nitentes,
Dum super in niveosque sinus iramque genarum
Excubias agerent immoto lumina vultu,
'Te colito: te nosce ipsum:'—(sic casta Dearum)—
'Te regito: hac itur summi ad fastigia regni.
Nec tamen hunc libeat sectando quærere finem:
Sponte aderit. Sapiens unus, cui ponere rectam
Vivendi steterit normam, qui ducere norit

And, because right is right, to follow right,
Were wisdom in the scorn of consequence.'
"Dear mother Ida, hearken ere I die!
Again she said: 'I woo thee not with gifts.
Sequel of guerdon could not alter me
To fairer. Judge thou me by what I am,
So shalt thou find me fairest.
Yet, indeed,
If, gazing on divinity disrobed,
Thy mortal eyes are frail to judge of fair,
Unbiass'd with self-profit, oh! rest thee sure
That I shall love thee well and cleave to thee,
So that my vigour, wedded to thy blood,
Shall strike within thy pulses like a god's,
To push thee forward thro' a life of shocks,
Dangers, and deeds, until endurance grow
Sinew'd with action, and the fullgrown will,
Circled thro' all experiences, pure law,
Commeasure perfect freedom.'
"Here she ceased;
And Paris pondered, and I cried, 'O Paris,
Give it to Pallas!' but he heard me not,
Or hearing would not hear me, woe is me!

Venturi impavidum securus temporis ævum.'

"Ida meam, genitrix, mors advenit, accipe vocem.
Deinde: 'Nec illecebris frustra deflectere litem
Constitui. Mea non adjecto munere forma
Clarior eniteat. Quod sum pulcherrima, per me
Ipsa probo.
Sed et oh! si contemplata Dearum
Nudatam speciem, vincat mortalia iniquum
Lumina judicium—si fas est fallere lucro—
Me tibi polliceor. Vegetos tibi detur amores
Abdita per cordis rapere, interiusque medullis
Illapsam sentire Deam. Sic crescet agendo,
Quicquid eris, duræ per spreta pericula vitæ,
Vis assueta pati, et tandem matura voluntas
Liberaque et sibimet lex impolluta vigebit.'

"Dixit: et hærentem dubio certamine mentem
Urgebam Paridi: 'Pallas tibi præmia, Pallas
Occupet!' Ah miseræ vanos confessa dolores!
Noluit, an nequiit, supremam audire querelam?

"O mother Ida, many-fountain'd Ida,
Dear mother Ida, hearken ere I die!
Idalian Aphrodite beautiful,
Fresh as the foam, new-bath'd in Paphian wells,
With rosy slender fingers backward drew
From her warm brows and bosom her deep hair
Ambrosial, golden round her lucid throat
And shoulder: from the violets her light foot
Shone rosy-white, and o'er her rounded form,
Between the shadows of the vine-bunches,
Floated the glowing sunlight, as she moved.
"Dear mother Ida, hearken ere I die!
She, with a subtle smile in her mild eye,
The herald of her triumph drawing nigh,
Half-whisper'd in his ear, 'I promise thee
The fairest and most loving wife in Greece.'
She spoke and laugh'd: I shut my sight for fear:
But when I look'd, Paris had raised his arm,
And I beheld great Here's angry eyes,
As she withdrew into the golden cloud,
And I was left alone within the bower:
And from that time to this I am alone,
And I shall be alone until I die.

"Me miseram exaudi scatebroso a culmine, mater!
Ida meam, genitrix, mors advenit, accipe vocem.
Ambrosia collum atque humeros aurata decoros
Cæsarie, roseo gracilis quam dextra retorsit
Innexam digito, pectus frontemque revelans,
Prodiit Idalia e Paphiæ modo fontibus undæ
Exoriens, spumæ similis Cytherea parenti:
Ad motum, tenues mistisque ruboribus albi
E violis micuere pedes, teretesque per artus
Vitibus incertas super intexentibus umbras,
Phœbei rutilam radii diffundere lucem.

"Ida meam, genitrix, mors advenit, accipe vocem.
Mox Dea, fatidico in caput inclinata susurro,
Jam victrix, placidoque arridens subdola vultu,
'Sponsam polliceor: qua sit nec amantior ulla,
Nec formam in Danais æque spectanda puellis.'
Nec plura, et risit. Mihi defecere paventi
Lumina. Suspiciens, Paridis cedentia vidi
Brachia, Junonemque aspectu torva minantem,
Aurea ut involvit nubes. Ego sola manebam:
Sola gemo: solam mors exoptata levabit.

"Yet, mother Ida, hearken ere I die!
Fairest—why fairest wife? Am I not fair?
My love hath told me so a thousand times.
Methinks I must be fair, for yesterday,
When I pass'd by, a wild and wanton pard,
Eyed like the evening star, with playful tail,
Crouch'd fawning in the weed. Most loving is she?
Ah me, my mountain shepherd, that my arms
Were wound about thee, and my hot lips prest
Close, close to thine, in that quick-falling dew
Of fruitful kisses, that as Autumn rains
Flash in the pools of whirling Simois.

"O mother, hear me yet, before I die!
They came, they cut away my tallest pines,
My dark, tall pines, that plumed the craggy ledge
High over the blue gorge, and all between
The snowy peak and snow-white cataract
Foster'd the callow eaglet—from beneath
Whose thick mysterious boughs, in the dark morn,
The panther's roar came muffled, as I sat
Low in the valley. Never, never more
Shall lone Œnone see the morning mist

"Ida tamen, genitrix, mors advenit, accipe vocem.
Scilicet et forma superat? Sed nec mihi formam
Deesse puer per mille vices iterare solebat.
Quinetiam pardus nuper mihi visus eunti
Blanditiis (mirum) insolitis, oculosque coruscus
Hesperio velut astra polo, per gramina lente
Ludere mulcendo, et pedibus subvolvere caudam.
Suavior at, dulces melius quæ discat amores?
Ah, mihi deliciæ! mea si te brachia cingant
Implicitum complexa! O si flagrantia detur
Oscula delibare iterumque iterumque labellis,
Æmula continui roris, qualisve coruscat
Multus in autumno Xanthi torrentibus imber!
"Extremam, genitrix, mors advenit, accipe vocem.
Tum cæsæ periere mihi, mea gaudia, pinus,
Queis in cœruleam super impendentibus olim
Convallem, in foliis nemorosæ rupis, et inter
Montanasque nives niveæque voraginis æstum,
Aeriis aquilæ prolem fovere latebris:
Unde, per horrentem cæca caligine frondem,
Nocte sub incerta, procul ima in valle sedenti
Panthera impulerat surdis mugitibus aurem.
Non ibi, non posthac, mea per pineta vapores

Sweep thro' them: never see them overlaid
With narrow moonlit strips of silver cloud,
Between the loud stream and the trembling stars.
"O mother, hear me yet before I die!
I wish that somewhere in the ruin'd folds,
Among the fragments tumbled from the glens,
Or the dry thickets, I could meet with her,
The Abominable, that uninvited came
Into the fair Peleian banquet-hall,
And cast the golden fruit upon the board,
And bred this change: that I might speak my mind,
And tell her, to her face, how much I hate
Her presence, hated both of gods and men.
"O mother, hear me yet before I die!
Hath he not sworn his love a thousand times,
In this green valley, under this green hill,
Ev'n on this hand, and sitting on this stone?
Seal'd it with kisses? water'd it with tears?
O happy tears, and how unlike to these!
O happy heaven, how canst thou see my face?
O happy earth, how canst thou bear my weight?
O death, death, death, thou ever floating cloud,
There are enough unhappy on this earth,

Radere iter rapidum prima sub luce videbo:
Nec tremulas inter stellas laticesque sonoros
Argentea tenues tinget face Cynthia nubes.
  " Extremam, genitrix, mors advenit, accipe vocem.
Illa mihi in dumis Infanda arentibus olim,
Fragmina vel scopulum, sive inter ovilia dudum
Deserta, occurrat, quæ Dis apud atria Pelei
Invitis epulas injecto miscuit auro,
Hasque mihi fecit lacrymas: sic impia demum
Audiat, et nobis et Dis invisa supremis.

  " Extremam, genitrix, mors advenit, accipe vocem.
Nonne mihi toties, hac ipsa in valle sedenti
Ad lapidem, perque hanc dextram, juravit amorem,
Osculaque et fido lacrymæ sanxere sigillo?
Heu quales recolo amissa dulcedine fletus!
Felices agri, vosque, o felicia testor
Sidera, me nimium et vanas perpessa querelas!
Mors eheu! mors assidua mortalibus umbra
Involitans! satis est miserum tibi copia prædæ;

Pass by the happy souls, that love to live:
I pray thee, pass before my light of life,
And shadow all my soul, that I may die.
Thou weighest heavy on the heart within,
Weigh heavy on my eyelids: let me die.
"O mother, hear me yet before I die!
I will not die alone, for fiery thoughts
Do shape themselves within me, more and more,
Whereof I catch the issue, as I hear
Dead sounds at night come from the inmost hills,
Like footsteps upon wool. I dimly see
My far-off doubtful purpose, as a mother
Conjectures of the features of her child
Ere it is born: her child!—a shudder comes
Across me: never child be born of me,
Unblest, to vex me with his father's eyes!
"O mother, hear me yet before I die!
Hear me, O earth! I will not die alone,
Lest their shrill, happy laughter come to me,
Walking the cold and starless road of death
Uncomforted, leaving my ancient love
With the Greek woman. I will rise, and go
Down into Troy, and, ere the stars come forth,

Ne tu felices animas, queis vivere dulce est,
Præripias: hanc invisæ mihi lampada vitæ
Conde tenebrosæ involvens caligine noctis.
Corda diu penitus te persensere receptam—
Pressa sit haud alio componere lumina leto.

"Extremam, genitrix, mors advenit, accipe vocem.
Non ego Lethæas ibo incomitata per undas:
Namque mihi, arcanis si quando oriuntur inanes
Montibus, ut pressa in tacitam vestigia lanam,
Nocte soni, fervet dubii mens præscia fati.
Auguror incertum facinus, ceu conscia mater
Visa sibi ignotæ formam prænoscere prolis:
—Ut dixi, ut tremui! Ne sit peperisse, paternum
Qui referat vana male natus imagine vultum!

"Extremam, genitrix, mors advenit, accipe vocem.
Terra, audi! Stygias non ibo sola per undas,
Neve mihi, gelidæ tenebroso in tramite mortis,
Arguto illudant, nullo solamine, risu,
Linquenti veteres Graia cum pellice amores.
Troja mihi quærenda. Velim surgentibus astris

Talk with the wild Cassandra, for she says
A fire dances before her, and a sound
Rings ever in her ears of armed men.
What this may be, I know not; but I know
That, whereso'er I am, by night and day,
All earth and air seem only burning fire."

ALFRED TENNYSON.

Cassandram affari: cui volvitur ignea semper
Ante oculos species, sonat indefessus in aures
Nescio quis belli clangor. Mihi nocte dieque
Ardent perpetuæ terram per et æthera flammæ."

L. 1857.

Godiva.

Not only we, the latest seed of Time,
New men, that in the flying of a wheel
Cry down the past; not only we, that prate
Of rights and wrongs, have lov'd the people well,
And loath'd to see them over-tax'd: but she
Did more, and underwent, and overcame,
The woman of a thousand summers back,
Godiva, wife to that grim Earl, who rul'd
In Coventry: for when he laid a tax
Upon his town, and all the mothers brought
Their children, clam'ring, "If we pay, we starve!"
She sought her lord, and found him where he strode
About the hall, among his dogs, alone,
His beard a foot before him, and his hair
A yard behind. She told him of their tears,
And pray'd him, "If they pay this tax, they starve!"
Whereat he star'd, replying, half-amaz'd,
"You would not let your little finger ache
For such as these?" "But I would die," said she.
He laugh'd, and swore by Peter and by Paul:

Scilicet oppressas sub iniquo pondere gentes
Nos, genus obscurum, durique novissima sæcli
Progenies, queis jura placent, qui spernimus annos
Præteritos, uni colere et miserescere demum
Novimus? At famæ victrix melioris honorem
Retulit, antiquum spectabilis illa per ævum
Huc usque, immitis conjux Godiva tyranni,
Cui morem gessere tui, Conventria, cives.
  Quæ, simul imposito (aiebant) peritura tributo
Affluere, et miseros visa est ostendere natos
Matrum turba loquax, dirum exorare maritum
Constituit. Regem spatiantem gressibus amplis,
Stipatum canibus, solaque invenit in aula.
Illum barba ingens anteibat, et horrida retro
Cæsaries longe tremulas fluitabat in auras.
Cui supplex, ægro ut gemeret plebecula fletu,
Venturamque famem, atque novi mala multa tributi,
Narrabat.
              Torvo paulum miratus ocello,
"Tune velis vel tantillum perferre laboris
Ne doleant isti?" "Quin et periisse," reponit.
Tum ridens, geminumque obtestans numina Divum,

Then fillip'd at the diamond in her ear;
"O ay, ay, ay, you talk!" "Alas!" she said,
"But prove me what it is I would not do."
And from a heart as rough as Esau's hand
He answer'd, "Ride you naked thro' the town,
And I repeal it:" and nodding, as in scorn,
He parted, with great strides among his dogs.
So left alone, the passions of her mind,
As winds from all the compass shift and blow,
Made war upon each other for an hour,
Till pity won.
She sent an herald forth,
And bid him cry, with sound of trumpet, all
Her hard condition; but that she would loose
The people: therefore, as they lov'd her well,
From then till noon no foot should pace the street,
No eye look down, she passing; but that all
Should keep within, door shut, and window barr'd.
Then fled she to her inmost bower, and there
Unclasp'd the wedded eagles of her belt,
The grim Earl's gift: but ever at a breath
She linger'd, looking like a summer moon
Half-dipt in cloud: anon she shook her head,
And shower'd the rippled ringlets to her knee:

"Nugæ adeo: mera verba!" refert: digitoque lacessens
Impulit insignem gemmis pendentibus aurem.
"Experiare modo!" et lacrymas celabat obortas.
At regi obriguere joco corda aspera sævo:
Annuit illudens: "Urbis tu nuda pererra
Compita: clamantes redimas hoc pignore cives:"
Hæc ille: erupitque ferox, canibusque coactis.
  Flabra per immensum ceu debacchantia cœlum,
Non aliter furere, et dubia contendere rixa,
Fœminei motus animi. Mox ipsa sibi ipsi
Cedit debellata. Amplam qui transeat urbem
Præconem emittit, duri et mandata tyranni
Inque suos magnum dominæ testetur amorem.
Proinde, "Ita qualiacunque mihi donata rependent,
Si plateis omnes vacuis, clausisque fenestris
Et foribus, maneant intra sua limina cives,
Donec Sol medium cœli conscenderit axem."
  Continuo ad thalami rapido penetralia gressu
Aufugit: zonæque, aquilas imitata gemellas,
Vincula secernit, truculenti dona tyranni;
Sæpe tamen dubio pendens, qualisque vaporem
Induit æstivas partim velata sub horas
Luna. Redundantes genibus tenus inde capillos

Unclad herself in haste: adown the stair
Stole on: and like a creeping sunbeam, slid
From pillar unto pillar, till she reach'd
The gateway: there she found her palfrey trapt
With purple blazon'd with armorial gold.
Then she rode forth, cloth'd on with chastity:
The deep air listen'd round her as she rode,
And all the low wind hardly breath'd for fear.
The little wide-mouth'd heads upon the spout
Had cunning eyes to see: the barking cur
Made her cheek flame: her palfrey's footfall shot
Light horrors thro' her pulses: the blind walls
Were full of chinks and holes: and overhead
Fantastic gables, crowding, star'd: but she
Not less thro' all bore up, till, last, she saw
The white-flower'd elder-thicket from the field
Gleam thro' the Gothic archways in the wall.
Then she rode back, cloth'd on with chastity:
And one low churl, compact of thankless earth,
The fatal byword of all years to come,
Boring a little auger-hole in fear
Peep'd—but his eyes, before they had their will,
Were shrivell'd into darkness in his head,
And dropt before him. So the Pow'rs, who wait

Excussit: trepida exutum deponit amictum:
Perque columnarum spatia anfractusque domorum,
Ut tacita in murum Solis subrepit imago,
Delapsa, ad limen vastique extrema palati
Venit. Stabat ibi sonipes, dominamque manebat,
Purpureis proavum signis auroque decorus.
Prodiit; et vestem suscepit nuda Pudorem.
At circum intenti pavido vix murmure venti
Spirare: effigies sculptæque in fonte figuræ
Vafris visæ oculis inhiare: canumque ululatu
Exarsere genæ. Quin et pede lenta caballi
Corda resultanti tremore, et levis horror in artus
Irruere: in cæco multas sibi pariete fraudes
Fingere per tenebras fissique foramina muri:
Et super insolitæ facies cuneique domorum
Undique miratum glomerarier. Illa tenebat
Indefessa viam. Tandem lustraverat urbem:
Incurvas tetigit portas, dumetaque vernis
Floribus in tacito videt albescentia prato.
Tum redit: et vestem prætendit nuda Pudorem.
At fuit infamis quidam de fæce popelli,
Terrarum sordes, et in omne ignobilis ævum,
Qui trepide et fatis murum terebraret iniquis,
Visurus. Sed enim Superi, qui magna tuentur

On noble deeds, cancell'd a sense misus'd:
And she, that knew not, pass'd: and all at once,
With twelve great shocks of sound, the shameless noon
Was clash'd and hammer'd from a hundred tow'rs,
One after one: but even then she gain'd
Her bower: whence reissuing, rob'd and crown'd,
To meet her lord, she took the tax away,
And built herself an everlasting name.

Ausa hominum, instabant vigiles: et cassa nefandi
Propositi subitæ tabi excæcata sacrarunt
Lumina. At illa redux thalamo intemerata resedit:
Raucisonoque fragore et centum e turribus una
Ora repercusso multum ingeminata tumultu
Flammantem intonuere poli super ardua Phæbum.
Deinde suo fastu et proprio diademate cincta
Egreditur, regemque petit: votoque potita
Condidit æternum ventura in sæcula nomen.

L. 1860.

Ulysses.

It little profits that an idle king,
By this still hearth, among these barren crags
Match'd with an aged wife, I mete and dole
Unequal laws unto a savage race,
That hoard, and sleep, and feed, and know not me.
I cannot rest from travel; I will drink
Life to the lees; all times I have enjoy'd
Greatly, all suffer'd greatly, both with those
That loved me, and alone; on shore and when
Thro' scudding drifts the rainy Hyades
Vext the dim sea: I am become a name;
For always roaming with a hungry heart
Much have I seen and known; cities of men,
And manners, climates, councils, governments,
Myself not least, but honour'd of them all;
And drunk delight of battle with my peers,
Far on the ringing plains of windy Troy.
I am a part of all that I have met;
Yet all experience is an arch wherethro'
Gleams that untravell'd world, whose margin fades
For ever and for ever as I move.
How dull it is to pause, to make an end,
To rust unburnish'd, not to shine in use!

Quid prodest? sterilis si languet inertia regni,
Adque Lares tacitos, effœta conjuge, leges
Metior incertas. Plebi sua vilia curæ;
Cogere rem, facilesque inter fera prandia somni;
Non ego. Quin iterum longarum ignota viarum
Ambire, et vitæ totos haurire labores,
Constituo. Solus, seu dulces inter amicos
Suavia permistos quoties solata dolores
Expertus recolo! Multæ per litora terræ
Notus ego, aut rapida freta percurrente procella,
Qua pluviis Hyadum vexantur marmora signis.
Cordis inexpleti impulerant jejunia, ut urbes
Et soles varios, cœtus, moresque viderem
Bellipotens; interque pares laudabile nomen
Æquora ventosæ norunt resonantia Trojæ.
Quidquid erat, pars ipse fui. Tamen allicit usque
Intactæ species terræ, et per temporis acta
Præteriti veluti portam translucet apertam:
Vana recedentis sequimur confinia campi.
Me vacui tædet, perfunctum munere, regni.
Splendet qui satagit: robigo fœdat inertem.

As tho' to breathe were life. Life piled on life
Were all too little, and of one to me
Little remains: but every hour is saved
From that eternal silence, something more,
A bringer of new things; and vile it were
For some three suns to store and hoard myself,
And this gray spirit yearning in desire
To follow knowledge, like a sinking star,
Beyond the utmost bound of human thought.
  This is my son, mine own Telemachus,
To whom I leave the sceptre and the isle—
Well-loved of me, discerning to fulfil
This labour, by slow prudence to make mild
A rugged people, and thro' soft degrees
Subdue them to the useful and the good.
Most blameless is he, centred in the sphere
Of common duties, decent not to fail
In offices of tenderness, and pay
Meet adoration to my household gods,
When I am gone. He works his work, I mine.
  There lies the port; the vessel puffs her sail;
There gloom the dark broad seas. My mariners,
Souls that have toil'd, and wrought, and thought with me,
That ever with a frolic welcome took

Qui spirat, vivit? Me sæclis addita sæcla,
Unius angusto contractum limite vitæ,
Deficerent. Sed enim labentia tempora Lethe
Præripit, ignotæque æterna silentia noctis.
Proinde nova aggredior. Pudet arctæ parcere vitæ:
Scire lubet quodcunque licet: crudaque senecta
Humanæ vetitos sophiæ transcendere fines,
Conditur extremas fugiens ut stella sub undas.

Ille mihi meus est, cui terram et sceptra remitto,
Telemachus: duce quo tardos mansuescat in annos
Gens ignara boni, et sollerti ducta magistro
Paullatim quid sit pulchrum, quid et utile, discat.
Scilicet innocuæ versatur tramite vitæ,
Debita seu patriis persolvit munera Divis,
Sive suos inter, totoque e corde, quietis
Deditur officiis. Porro sua cuique laboris
Præmia. Me portus, me pleno carbasa vento,
Cœruleique vocant ingentia marmora ponti.
Vosque, senescentes mecum, mea gaudia, nautæ,
Quidquid consului comites, sociique laborum,
Vos hilari fronte et generoso pectore fortes

The thunder and the sunshine, and opposed
Free hearts, free foreheads, you and I are old;
Old age hath yet his honour and his toil;
Death closes all; but something ere the end,
Some work of noble note, may yet be done,
Not unbecoming men that strove with gods.
  The lights began to twinkle from the rocks:
The long day wanes: the slow moon climbs: the deep
Moans round with many voices. Come, my friends,
'Tis not too late to seek a newer world.
Push off, and sitting well in order smite
The sounding furrows; for my purpose holds
To sail beyond the sunset, and the baths
Of all the western stars, until I die.
It may be that the gulfs will wash us down:
It may be we shall touch the happy Isles,
And see the great Achilles, whom we knew.
Tho' much is taken, much abides; and tho'
We are not now that strength which in old days
Moved earth and heaven: that which we are, we are;
One equal temper of heroic hearts,
Made weak by time and fate, but strong in will
To strive, to seek, to find, and not to yield.

TENNYSON.

Fulmineas inter nubes, vel sole serenum
Tranquillante polum,—superest et fama senectæ.
Mors homini finis rerum. Laus ultima vitæ
Nobile sit quiddam facinus, nos quale decebat
Ausos vel Superis infandum intendere bellum.
At vespertinæ e scopulis lucescere tædæ:
Lentaque cunctantis venit in vestigia Phœbi
Cynthia: multisoni circum gemit Oceani vox.
Ergo alii nobis tractus, aliæque, sodales,
Quarendæ gentes; pulsaque a littore cymba
Ordine composito resonantes verrite sulcos.
Stat super Hesperios fines Solisque cubile,
Siderum ubi gelidis agmen restinguitur undis,
Pergere navigio, dum spiritus hos regit artus.
Deinde procelloso pelagus seu volvat in æstu,
Sive ad Achilleam (nobis quoque notus Achilles)
Sors ducat melior, campis felicibus, umbram,
Nonnihil e reliquo fas sit lucrarier ævo.
Nos fati insidiæ, nos imbecillior ætas
Affligit: neque nunc ea vis, mortalibus olim
Et superis metuenda. Sumus tamen: æqua piorum
Corda virum, quibus unus amor, stabilisque voluntas
Invictis positam nitendo attingere metam.

L. 1862.

TRANSLATIONS

BY THE

RIGHT HON. W. E. GLADSTONE.

The Lion's Cub.

AGAM. 696—716.

STR. II.

ἔθρεψεν δὲ λέοντα
σίνιν δόμοις ἀγάλακτον οὕ-
τως ἀνὴρ φιλόμαστον·
ἐν βιότου προτελείοις
ἅμερον, εὐφιλόπαιδα,
καὶ γεραροῖς ἐπίχαρτον.
πολέα δ' ἔσκ' ἐν ἀγκάλαις,
νεοτρόφου τέκνου δίκαν,
φαιδρωπὸς ποτὶ χεῖρα, σαί-
νων τε γαστρὸς ἀνάγκαις.

ANTISTR. II.

χρονισθεὶς δ' ἀπέδειξεν
ἔθος τὸ πρὸς τοκέων· χάριν
γὰρ τροφεῦσιν ἀμείβων
μηλοφόνοισιν ἄγαισιν
δαῖτ' ἀκέλευστος ἔτευξεν·
αἵματι δ' οἶκος ἐφύρθη,
ἄμαχον ἄλγος οἰκέταις,
μέγα σίνος πολυκτόνον.
ἐκ θεοῦ δ' ἱερεύς τις Ἄ-
τας δόμοις προσεθρέφθη.

Even so, belike, might one
A lion suckling nurse,
Like a foster-son,
To his home a future curse.
In life's beginnings mild,
Dear to sire, and kind to child;
Oft folded in his lord's embrace,
Like an infant of the race.
Sleek and smiling to the hand,
He fawned at want's command.

But in time he showed
The habit of his blood:
His debt of nurture he repaid;
The lowing herds he tore,
A fierce unbidden feast he made,
And the house was foul with gore.
Huge grief its inmates overshed,
Huge mischief, slaughter widely spread!
A heaven-sent Priest of Woe
In the Palace did he grow.

1836.

From the Homeric Hymn to the Delian Apollo.

165—178.

Ἀλλ' ἄγεθ', ἱλήκοι μὲν Ἀπόλλων Ἀρτέμιδι ξὺν,
χαίρετε δ' ὑμεῖς πᾶσαι· ἐμεῖο δὲ καὶ μετόπισθεν
μνήσασθ', ὁππότε κέν τις ἐπιχθονίων ἀνθρώπων
ἐνθάδ' ἀνείρηται ξεῖνος ταλαπείριος ἐλθών·
ὦ κοῦραι, τίς δ' ὔμμιν ἀνὴρ ἥδιστος ἀοιδῶν
ἐνθάδε πωλεῖται, καὶ τέῳ τέρπεσθε μάλιστα;
ὑμεῖς δ' εὖ μάλα πᾶσαι ὑποκρίνασθ' εὐφήμως·
τυφλὸς ἀνὴρ, οἰκεῖ δὲ Χίῳ ἐνὶ παιπαλοέσσῃ·
τοῦ πᾶσαι μετόπισθεν ἀριστεύουσιν ἀοιδαί.
ἡμεῖς δ' ὑμέτερον κλεὸς οἴσομεν, ὅσσον ἐπ' αἶαν
ἀνθρώπων στρεφόμεσθα πόλεις εὐναιεταώσας·
οἱ δ' ἐπὶ δὴ πείσονται, ἐπεὶ καὶ ἐτήτυμόν ἐστιν.
αὐτὰρ ἐγὼν οὐ λήξω ἑκηβόλον Ἀπόλλωνα
ὑμνέων ἀργυρότοξον, ὃν ἠΰκομος τέκε Λητώ.

THEN Artemis with thee, Apollo, smile!
Daughters, fare ye well the while;
Me too remember, when
From among the sons of men
Some wayworn stranger shall inquire
As he journeys by:
"Whom of the vocal choir,
O damsels, do ye most desire?
Who sweetliest strikes the lyre?"
Then auspiciously,
Then with one accord reply:
"The blind old man, that dwells in high
And rocky Chios, he is dear;
Him we most delight to hear;
All his deathless verse
Distant ages shall rehearse."
I in turn will bear your fame
Far as over earth I go,
Through cities of renowned name;
And they shall know
It is the truth that I proclaim.
Nor will I cease to sing
The silver-bowed far-darting King,
Whom Leto bare,
Leto, with flowing hair.

1836.

The Battle of the Fourth Book.

Il. IV. 422—443.

Ὡς δ' ὅτ' ἐν αἰγιαλῷ πολυηχέϊ κῦμα θαλάσσης
Ὄρνυτ' ἐπασσύτερον, Ζεφύρου ὑποκινήσαντος·
Πόντῳ μὲν τὰ πρῶτα κορύσσεται, αὐτὰρ ἔπειτα
Χέρσῳ ῥηγνύμενον μεγάλα βρέμει, ἀμφὶ δέ τ' ἄκρας
Κυρτὸν ἐὸν κορυφοῦται, ἀποπτύει δ' ἁλὸς ἄχνην·
Ὣς τότ' ἐπασσύτεραι Δαναῶν κίνυντο φάλαγγες
Νωλεμέως πόλεμόνδε· κέλευε δὲ οἷσιν ἕκαστος
Ἡγεμόνων· οἱ δ' ἄλλοι ἀκὴν ἴσαν—οὐδέ κε φαίης
Τόσσον λαὸν ἕπεσθαι ἔχοντ' ἐν στήθεσιν αὐδὴν—
Σιγῇ δειδιότες σημάντορας· ἀμφὶ δὲ πᾶσι
Τεύχεα ποικίλ' ἔλαμπε, τὰ εἱμένοι ἐστιχόωντο.

As when the billow gathers fast
  With slow and sullen roar
Beneath the keen north-western blast
  Against the sounding shore:
First far at sea it rears its crest,
  Then bursts upon the beach,
Or with proud arch and swelling breast,
  Where headlands outward reach,
It smites their strength, and bellowing flings
  Its silver foam afar;
So, stern and thick, the Danaan kings
  And soldiers marched to war.
Each leader gave his men the word,
Each warrior deep in silence heard;
So mute they marched, thou could'st not ken
They were a mass of speaking men;
And as they strode, in martial might,
Their flickering arms shot back the light.

Τρῶες δ', ὥς τ' ὄϊες πολυπάμονος ἀνδρὸς ἐν αὐλῇ
Μυρίαι ἑστήκασιν ἀμελγόμεναι γάλα λευκὸν,
Ἀζηχὲς μεμακυῖαι, ἀκούουσαι ὄπα ἀρνῶν,
Ὣς Τρώων ἀλαλητὸς ἀνὰ στρατὸν εὐρὺν ὀρώρει·
Οὐ γὰρ πάντων ἦεν ὁμὸς θρόος οὐδ' ἴα γῆρυς,
Αλλὰ γλῶσσα μέμικτο, πολύκλητοι δ' ἔσαν ἄνδρες.
Ὦρσε δὲ τοὺς μὲν Ἄρης, τοὺς δὲ γλαυκῶπις Ἀθήνη,
Δεῖμός τ' ἠδὲ Φόβος καὶ Ἔρις ἄμοτον μεμαυῖα,
Ἄρεος ἀνδροφόνοιο κασιγνήτη ἑτάρη τε,
Η τ' ὀλίγη μὲν πρῶτα κορύσσεται, αὐτὰρ ἔπειτα
Οὐράνῳ ἐστήριξε κάρη, καὶ ἐπὶ χθονὶ βαίνει.

But, as at even the folded sheep
  Of some rich master stand,
Ten thousand thick their place they keep,
  And bide the milkman's hand,
And more and more they bleat, the more
  They hear their lamblings cry;
So from the Trojan host, uproar
  And din rose loud and high.
They were a many-voicèd throng;
  Discordant accents there,
That sound from many a differing tongue,
  Their differing race declare.
These, Ares kindled for the fight;
Those, starry-eyed Athenè's might,
And savage Terror, and Affright,
And Strife, of wars insatiate,
Sister of Ares, and his mate;
Strife that, a pigmy at her birth,
  By gathering rumour fed,
Soon plants her feet upon the earth
  And in the heaven her head.

1859.

Battle of the Eleventh Book.

Il. XI. 67—83.

Οἱ δ', ὥστ' ἀμητῆρες ἐνάντιοι ἀλλήλοισιν
Ὄγμον ἐλαύνουσιν, ἀνδρὸς μάκαρος κατ' ἄρουραν,
Πυρῶν, ἢ κριθῶν, τὰ δὲ δράγματα ταρφέα πίπτει·
Ὣς Τρῶες καὶ Ἀχαιοὶ ἐπ' ἀλλήλοισι θορόντες
Δῄουν, οὐδ' ἕτεροι μνώοντ' ὀλοοῖο φόβοιο·
Ἴσας δ' ὑσμίνη κεφαλὰς ἔχον· οἱ δὲ, λύκοι ὥς,
Θῦνον· Ἔρις δ' ἄρ' ἔχαιρε πολύστονος εἰσορόωσα·
Οἴη γάρ ῥα θεῶν παρετύγχανε μαρναμένοισιν·
Οἱ δ' ἄλλοι οὔ σφιν πάρεσαν θεοὶ, ἀλλὰ ἕκηλοι
Οἷσιν ἐνὶ μεγάροισι καθείατο· ἧχι ἑκάστῳ
Δώματα καλὰ τέτυκτο κατὰ πτύχας Οὐλύμποιο·
Πάντες δ' ᾐτιόωντο κελαινεφέα Κρονίωνα,
Οὕνεκ' ἄρα Τρώεσσιν ἐβούλετο κῦδος ὀρέξαι.
Τῶν μὲν ἄρ' οὐκ ἀλέγιζε πατήρ· ὁ δὲ, νόσφι λιασθεὶς,
Τῶν ἄλλων ἀπάνευθε καθέζετο κύδεϊ γαίων,
Εἰσορόων Τρώων τε πόλιν καὶ νῆας Ἀχαιῶν,
Χαλκοῦ τε στεροπὴν, ὀλλύντας τ', ὀλλυμένους τε.

As in some rich man's domain
  The reapers drawn in rows,
Right down the furrows shear the grain,
  And still their labour grows,
And thick the armfuls fall as rain;
So Trojan and Achaian might
  Each on the other leapt;
None turned from fight to cursèd flight,
  But even battle kept.
They raged like wolves. With deadly smile
Fell Strife sate lowering by the while;
She singly of the gods was there,
The rest abode in upper air;
Deep-valed Olumpos all enshrouds,
  Each in his beauteous palace calm,
Each blaming Zeus, the King of clouds,
  Who willed to Troy the victor's palm.
The Sire he held their murmurs light,
  And drawing far away,
He sate, exulting in his might,
  And overlooked the bay,
The ships of the Achaians,
  The city on the plain,
The flashing of the brazen arms,
  The slayers and the slain.

Note, that in this version of the First Book of the Iliad,

The Latin	JUPITER is . .	ZEUS . . .	also	KRONIDES, KRONĪON.
	JUNO	HERÈ.		
	MINERVA . . .	ATHENÈ.		
	APOLLO . . .	APOLLO . .	also	PHŒBUS, HECAERGOS, HECATOS.
	VULCAN . . .	HEPHAISTOS.		
	GREEKS . . .	ACHAIANS. .	also	ARGEIANS, DANAANS.
Also, that	ACHILLES or ACHILES	is likewise called . . .		PELĪDES, PELION.
	AGAMEMNON			ATRĪDES. ATRĪON.

Iliad.—Book I.

Μῆνιν ἄειδε, θεὰ, Πηληϊάδεω Ἀχιλῆος,
οὐλομένην, ἣ μυρί' Ἀχαιοῖς ἄλγε' ἔθηκεν,
πολλὰς δ' ἰφθίμους ψυχὰς Ἄϊδι προΐαψεν
ἡρώων, αὐτοὺς δὲ ἑλώρια τεῦχε κύνεσσιν
οἰωνοῖσί τε πᾶσι· Διὸς δ' ἐτελείετο βουλὴ,
ἐξ οὗ δὴ τὰ πρῶτα διαστήτην ἐρίσαντε
Ἀτρείδης τε, ἄναξ ἀνδρῶν, καὶ δῖος Ἀχιλλεύς.
Τίς τ' ἄρ σφῶε θεῶν ἔριδι ξυνέηκε μάχεσθαι ;
Λητοῦς καὶ Διὸς υἱός. ὁ γὰρ βασιλῆϊ χολωθεὶς
νοῦσον ἀνὰ στρατὸν ὦρσε κακὴν, ὀλέκοντο δὲ λαοὶ,
οὕνεκα τὸν Χρύσην ἠτίμησ' ἀρητῆρα
Ἀτρείδης. ὁ γὰρ ἦλθε θοὰς ἐπὶ νῆας Ἀχαιῶν,
λυσόμενός τε θύγατρα φέρων τ' ἀπερείσι' ἄποινα,
στέμματ' ἔχων ἐν χερσὶν ἑκηβόλου Ἀπόλλωνος,
χρυσέῳ ἀνὰ σκήπτρῳ, καὶ λίσσετο πάντας Ἀχαιοὺς,
Ἀτρείδα δὲ μάλιστα δύω, κοσμήτορε λαῶν·

Of Achilles, son of Peleus, how the deadly wrath arose;
How the host of the Achaians rued it with ten thousand woes;
How the wraiths of stalwart heroes Hades gat before his day,
Left themselves, for dogs to feed on, and for every bird of prey,
Sing, O Goddess! how all-ruling Zeus fulfilled his stedfast plan,
From the hour when, torn asunder, they, the twain, to strive began,
Agamemnon, lord of heroes, and Achilles, flower of man.

Who among the gods inflamed them, that the fatal feud outbroke?
'Twas the Son of Zeus with Leto. Toward the King his anger woke;
Through the host a Plague he kindled, and in thousands fell the folk.
For Atrides did dishonour unto Chryses, man of prayer,
When to the Achaian vessels store of endless gifts he bare
For the ransom of his daughter. In his hands the garlands were,
On the gold-wrought staff of Phœbus. Suppliant to the chiefs he spoke,
Most of all the two Atridai, the Commanders of the folk.

"'Ατρεΐδαί τε καὶ ἄλλοι ἐϋκνημῖδες 'Αχαιοὶ,
ὑμῖν μὲν θεοὶ δοῖεν 'Ολύμπια δώματ' ἔχοντες
ἐκπέρσαι Πριάμοιο πόλιν, εὖ δ' οἴκαδ' ἱκέσθαι·
παῖδα δ' ἐμοὶ λῦσαί τε φίλην τά τ' ἄποινα δέχεσθαι,
ἀζόμενοι Διὸς υἱὸν ἑκηβόλον 'Απόλλωνα."
"Ενθ' ἄλλοι μὲν πάντες ἐπευφήμησαν 'Αχαιοὶ
αἰδεῖσθαί θ' ἱερῆα καὶ ἀγλαὰ δέχθαι ἄποινα·
ἀλλ' οὐκ 'Ατρεΐδῃ 'Αγαμέμνονι ἥνδανε θυμῷ,
ἀλλὰ κακῶς ἀφίει, κρατερὸν δ' ἐπὶ μῦθον ἔτελλε·
" Μή σε, γέρον, κοίλῃσιν ἐγὼ παρὰ νηυσὶ κιχείω
ἢ νῦν δηθύνοντ' ἢ ὕστερον αὖτις ἰόντα,
μή νύ τοι οὐ χραίσμῃ σκῆπτρον καὶ στέμμα θεοῖο.
τὴν δ' ἐγὼ οὐ λύσω· πρίν μιν καὶ γῆρας ἔπεισιν
ἡμετέρῳ ἐνὶ οἴκῳ, ἐν Ἄργεϊ, τηλόθι πατρης,
ἱστὸν ἐποιχομένην καὶ ἐμὸν λέχος ἀντιόωσαν.
ἀλλ' ἴθι, μή μ' ἐρέθιζε, σαώτερος ὥς κε νέηαι."
"Ως ἔφατ'· ἔδδεισεν δ' ὁ γέρων καὶ ἐπείθετο μύθῳ.
βῆ δ' ἀκέων παρὰ θῖνα πολυφλοίσβοιο θαλάσσης.
πολλὰ δ' ἔπειτ' ἀπάνευθε κιὼν ἠρᾶθ' ὁ γεραιὸς
'Απόλλωνι ἄνακτι, τὸν ἠΰκομος τέκε Λητώ·
" Κλῦθί μευ, ἀργυρότοξ', ὃς Χρύσην ἀμφιβέβηκας
Κίλλαν τε ζαθέην Τενέδοιό τε ἶφι ἀνάσσεις,
Σμινθεῦ· εἴποτέ τοι χαρίεντ' ἐπὶ νηὸν ἔρεψα,
ἢ εἰ δή ποτέ τοι κατὰ πίονα μηρί' ἔκηα
ταύρων ἠδ' αἰγῶν, τόδε μοι κρήηνον ἐέλδωρ·

"Sons of Atreus, and your comrades, stoutly greaved Achaians all!
May the gods, that hold Olympus, grant it shall your host befall
Both to sack the town of Priam, and to see your homes again.
But release my darling daughter, and my proffered gifts retain,
Venerating great Apollo, son of Zeus, far-darting Lord.

Then Apollo's priest to honour all th' Achaians gave accord,
And to take the costly ransom: one, one only said him nay,
And with speech full rude and scornful drave the ancient man away;
Agamemnon, son of Atreus. "Neither, grey-beard, lag to-day,
Nor in aftertime returning be thou found about the strand,
Lest the staff should not avail thee, nor the garland in thine hand.
For the maiden, at my palace there in Argos she shall stay,
Till old age shall overtake her, from her father-land away.
There she still shall ply the distaff, there she still my bed shall share.
If thou wouldst depart in safety, stir me not; begone, beware."

So he spake. The old man trembled, and obeyed. Along the shore
Silently he paced, and listened to the sea's tumultuous roar.
When the camp lay all behind him, forth he poured his mind in prayer
To Apollo, Son of Leto, Leto with the flowing hair.

"Thou, that Chryse still protectest, that in Sminthe dost delight,
And in holiest Killa; thou that rulest Tenedos with might;
If mine hands for thy fair temple oftentimes have garlands wrought,
And have burned, for thee, the thigh-bones in their fat, of bull and goat;
Hear me, silver-bowed Apollo! hear, and answer what I pray;

τίσειαν Δαναοὶ ἐμὰ δάκρυα σοῖσι βέλεσσιν."
Ὣς ἔφατ' εὐχόμενος· τοῦ δ' ἔκλυε Φοῖβος Ἀπόλλων·
βῆ δὲ κατ' Οὐλύμποιο καρήνων χωόμενος κῆρ,
τόξ' ὤμοισιν ἔχων ἀμφηρεφέα τε φαρέτρην.
ἔκλαγξαν δ' ἄρ' ὀϊστοὶ ἐπ' ὤμων χωομένοιο,
αὐτοῦ κινηθέντος. ὁ δ' ἤϊε νυκτὶ ἐοικώς.
ἕζετ' ἔπειτ' ἀπάνευθε νεῶν, μετὰ δ' ἰὸν ἕηκε·
δεινὴ δὲ κλαγγὴ γένετ' ἀργυρέοιο βιοῖο.
οὐρῆας μὲν πρῶτον ἐπῴχετο καὶ κύνας ἀργούς,
αὐτὰρ ἔπειτ' αὐτοῖσι βέλος ἐχεπευκὲς ἐφιεὶς
βάλλ'· αἰεὶ δὲ πυραὶ νεκύων καίοντο θαμειαί.
Ἐννῆμαρ μὲν ἀνὰ στρατὸν ᾤχετο κῆλα θεοῖο,
τῇ δεκάτῃ δ' ἀγορήνδε καλέσσατο λαὸν Ἀχιλλεύς·
τῷ γὰρ ἐπὶ φρεσὶ θῆκε θεὰ λευκώλενος Ἥρη·
κήδετο γὰρ Δαναῶν, ὅτι ῥα θνήσκοντας ὁρᾶτο.
οἱ δ' ἐπεὶ οὖν ἤγερθεν ὁμηγερέες τ' ἐγένοντο,
τοῖσι δ' ἀνισταμενος μετέφη πόδας ὠκὺς Ἀχιλλεύς·
"Ἀτρείδη, νῦν ἄμμε παλιμπλαγχθέντας ὀΐω
ἂψ ἀπονοστήσειν, εἴ κεν θάνατόν γε φύγοιμεν,
εἰ δὴ ὁμοῦ πόλεμός τε δαμᾷ καὶ λοιμὸς Ἀχαιούς.
ἀλλ' ἄγε δή τινα μάντιν ἐρείομεν, ἢ ἱερῆα,
ἢ καὶ ὀνειροπόλον—καὶ γάρ τ' ὄναρ ἐκ Διός ἐστιν—
ὅς κ' εἴποι ὅ τι τόσσον ἐχώσατο Φοῖβος Ἀπόλλων,
εἴτ' ἄρ' ὅγ' εὐχωλῆς ἐπιμέμφεται εἴθ' ἑκατόμβης,
αἴ κέν πως ἀρνῶν κνίσσης αἰγῶν τε τελείων

By thine arrows let the Danaans for my tears requital pay!"

So he prayed. Apollo Phœbus heard his prayer. With anger stung
From the summits of Olympus straight in downward course he flung.
With his bow, upon his shoulder all-compact his quiver hung;
As he swept along like nightfall in his scorn, his arrows rung.
Then he sate, the fleet beholding from afar; then shot the dart.
Loudly clangs the bow of silver, as the bitter arrows start
First the mules and hounds quick-footed, then the host of men to slay.
Funeral pyres are flaming upward, thicker still from day to day.

Nine the days those darts from heaven through the army scattered fate;
But upon the tenth, Achilles called the people to debate.
White-armed Herè so inspired him, grieving for the Danaan dead.
When they met, and all were gathered, swift Achilles rose, and said.

"Son of Atreus, it were better we should seek our homes afar
While we may, than thus to perish stricken both by Plague and War.
At the least, to ask some prophet, or some priest will well beseem,
Or some sage dream-teller, seeing that 'tis Zeus who gives the dream.
Such may teach us, why Apollo is in anger and in gloom;
Is it lack of hymns he charges, is it stinted hecatomb?
If perchance of goats unblemished and of lambs the savour may

βούλεται ἀντιάσας ἡμῖν ἀπὸ λοιγὸν ἀμῦναι."
"Ητοι ὅγ' ὣς εἰπὼν κατ' ἄρ' ἕζετο. τοῖσι δ' ἀνέστη
Κάλχας Θεστορίδης, οἰωνοπόλων ὄχ' ἄριστος,
ὃς ᾔδη τά τ' ἐόντα τά τ' ἐσσόμενα πρό τ' ἐόντα,
καὶ νήεσσ' ἡγήσατ' 'Αχαιῶν "Ιλιον εἴσω,
ἣν διὰ μαντοσύνην, τήν οἱ πόρε Φοῖβος 'Απόλλων·
ὅ σφιν ἐϋφρονέων ἀγορήσατο καὶ μετέειπεν
"'Ω 'Αχιλεῦ, κέλεαί με, Διὶ φίλε, μυθήσασθαι
μῆνιν 'Απόλλωνος, ἑκατηβελέταο ἄνακτος.
τοιγὰρ ἐγὼν ἐρέω· σὺ δὲ σύνθεο καί μοι ὄμοσσον
ἦ μέν μοι πρόφρων ἔπεσιν καὶ χερσὶν ἀρήξειν.
ἦ γὰρ ὀΐομαι ἄνδρα χολωσέμεν, ὃς μέγα πάντων
'Αργείων κρατέει καί οἱ πείθονται 'Αχαιοί.
κρείσσων γὰρ βασιλεὺς, ὅτε χώσεται ἀνδρὶ χέρηϊ·
εἴπερ γάρ τε χόλον γε καὶ αὐτῆμαρ καταπέψῃ,
ἀλλά τε καὶ μετόπισθεν ἔχει κότον, ὄφρα τελέσσῃ,
ἐν στήθεσσιν ἑοῖσι. σὺ δὲ φράσαι εἴ με σαώσεις."
Τὸν δ' ἀπαμειβόμενος προσέφη πόδας ὠκὺς 'Αχιλλεύς·
" θαρσήσας μάλα εἰπὲ θεοπρόπιον ὅ τι οἶσθα.
οὐ μὰ γὰρ 'Απόλλωνα Διὶ φίλον, ᾧτε σὺ, Κάλχαν,
εὐχόμενος Δαναοῖσι θεοπροπίας ἀναφαίνεις,
οὔτις ἐμεῦ ζῶντος καὶ ἐπὶ χθονὶ δερκομένοιο
σοὶ κοίλῃς παρὰ νηυσὶ βαρείας χεῖρας ἐποίσει
συμπάντων Δαναῶν, οὐδ' ἢν 'Αγαμέμνονα εἴπῃς,
ὃς νῦν πολλὸν ἄριστος 'Αχαιῶν εὔχεται εἶναι."

Yet avail us, and fell ruin from the army ward away."

He had ended. Then rose Calchas, son of Thestor; best of seers,
For he knew the past and present, and the things of coming years;
And the Danaan ships to Ilion he had guided o'er the wave
By the gift of prophet-vision, that Apollo Phœbus gave.
He in friendly tones addressed them.— "Dost thou bid me speak the cause
Why from far the Lord Apollo thus his bow for havock draws?
I will tell it, O Achilles, dear to Zeus. Yet first accord,
On thine oath, that thou shalt help me, help me both with deed and word.
For I trow my speech shall anger one, who wields a mighty sway
O'er the folk of the Argeians, and whom all the Chiefs obey.
Sure the King hath alway reason in contending with the vile;
And if even for the moment he shall well digest his bile,
Yet he bears the grudge thereafter, to fulfil another while.
Tell me; wilt thou save?" Achilles in his turn the Seer addressed.

"Speak, and fear not, whatsoever heav'n hath lodged within thy breast:
For, I swear it by Apollo dear to Zeus, whose high decrees,
Calchas, thou his votary tellest; while Achilles lives and sees,
None shall lay the hand upon thee, by the ships upon the coast,
No not were it Agamemnon, from among the Danaan host,
Though of all the bold Achaians to be far the first he boast."

Καὶ τότε δὴ θάρσησε καὶ ηὔδα μάντις ἀμύμων
"οὔτ' ἄρ' ὅγ' εὐχωλῆς ἐπιμέμφεται οὔθ' ἑκατόμβης,
ἀλλ' ἕνεκ' ἀρητῆρος, ὃν ἠτίμησ' Ἀγαμέμνων
οὐδ' ἀπέλυσε θύγατρα καὶ οὐκ ἀπεδέξατ' ἄποινα·
τοὔνεκ' ἄρ' ἄλγε' ἔδωκεν Ἑκηβόλος ἠδ' ἔτι δώσει.
οὐδ' ὅγε πρὶν Δαναοῖσιν ἀεικέα λοιγὸν ἀπώσει,
πρίν γ' ἀπὸ πατρὶ φίλῳ δόμεναι ἑλικώπιδα κούρην
ἀπριάτην, ἀνάποινον, ἄγειν θ' ἱερὴν ἑκατόμβην
ἐς Χρύσην· τότε κέν μιν ἱλασσάμενοι πεπίθοιμεν."
Ἤτοι ὅγ' ὣς εἰπὼν κατ' ἄρ' ἕζετο, τοῖσι δ' ἀνέστη
ἥρως Ἀτρείδης εὐρυκρείων Ἀγαμέμνων
ἀχνύμενος· μένεος δὲ μέγα φρένες ἀμφιμέλαιναι
πίμπλαντ', ὄσσε δέ οἱ πυρὶ λαμπετόωντι ἐΐκτην.
Κάλχαντα πρώτιστα κακ' ὀσσόμενος προσέειπεν·
"Μάντι κακῶν, οὐ πώποτέ μοι τὸ κρήγυον εἶπας.
αἰεί τοι τὰ κακ' ἐστὶ φίλα φρεσὶ μαντεύεσθαι,
ἐσθλὸν δ' οὔτε τί πω εἶπας ἔπος οὔτ' ἐτέλεσσας·
καὶ νῦν ἐν Δαναοῖσι θεοπροπέων ἀγορεύεις
ὡς δὴ τοῦδ' ἕνεκά σφιν Ἑκηβόλος ἄλγεα τεύχει,
οὕνεκ' ἐγὼ κούρης Χρυσηΐδος ἀγλα' ἄποινα
οὐκ ἔθελον δέξασθαι, ἐπεὶ πολὺ βούλομαι αὐτὴν
οἴκοι ἔχειν. καὶ γάρ ῥα Κλυταιμνήστρης προβέβουλα,
κουριδίης ἀλόχου, ἐπεὶ οὔ ἑθέν ἐστι χερείων,
οὐ δέμας οὐδὲ φυὴν, οὔτ' ἂρ φρένας οὔτε τι ἔργα.
ἀλλὰ καὶ ὣς ἐθέλω δόμεναι πάλιν, εἰ τόγ' ἄμεινον·

Then the noble Seer took courage, and declared the deadly doom.
" 'Tis not lack of hymns he charges, 'tis not stinted hecatomb.
'Tis because that Agamemnon put to shame the man of prayer,
Neither would release his daughter, neither take the ransom rare.
Hence the Archer hath decreed us woes, and will decree us more;
Nor will Phœbus stray from smiting with his weighty hand, before,
Ye without or fine or ransom give the maid of glancing eyes
To her father, and to Chryse bring the holy sacrifice.
So, we may appease Apollo." Calchas said, and sate again.
Rose Atrion Agamemnon, Hero widely ruling men;
Vexed, and all his darkling spirit charged with wrath, his eyes with flame;
First of all to Calchas, boding evil, words of anger came.
" Seer of ills! for never surely hast thou spoken for my weal!
Alway auguries of mischief thou delightest to reveal;
No, nor once the word of profit hast thou done me, neither spoke.
Now for oracle from heaven tellest thou the Danaan folk
That the Archer Phœbus vexeth them with sorrows for my sake,
For that I the priceless ransom of Chryseis shunned to take?
Surely I prefer to hold her at my home; for in mine eyes
Maiden-wedded Clytemnestra yet is not so dear a prize,
And excels her not in beauty, nature, sense, or useful art.
But to yield her I deny not, so it be the better part,

βούλομ' ἐγὼ λαὸν σῶν ἔμμεναι ἢ ἀπολέσθαι.
αὐτὰρ ἐμοὶ γέρας αὐτίχ' ἑτοιμάσατ', ὄφρα μὴ οἶος
'Αργείων ἀγέραστος ἔω, ἐπεὶ οὐδὲ ἔοικεν.
λεύσσετε γὰρ τόγε πάντες, ὅ μοι γέρας ἔρχεται ἄλλῃ."
Τὸν δ' ἠμείβετ' ἔπειτα ποδάρκης δῖος Ἀχιλλεύς
" 'Ατρείδη κύδιστε, φιλοκτεανώτατε πάντων,
πῶς γάρ τοι δώσουσι γέρας μεγάθυμοι Ἀχαιοί;
οὐδέ τί που ἴδμεν ξυνήϊα κείμενα πολλά·
ἀλλὰ τὰ μὲν πολίων ἐξ ἐπράθομεν, τὰ δέδασται,
λαοὺς δ' οὐκ ἐπέοικε παλίλλογα ταῦτ' ἐπαγείρειν.
ἀλλὰ σὺ μὲν νῦν τήνδε θεῷ πρόες· αὐτὰρ Ἀχαιοὶ
τριπλῇ τετραπλῇ τ' ἀποτίσομεν, αἴ κέ ποθι Ζεὺς
δῷσι πόλιν Τροίην εὐτείχεον ἐξαλάπαξαι."
Τὸν δ' ἀπαμειβόμενος προσέφη κρείων Ἀγαμέμνων
" μὴ δ' οὕτως, ἀγαθός περ ἐών, θεοείκελ' Ἀχιλλεῦ,
κλέπτε νόῳ, ἐπεὶ οὐ παρελεύσεαι οὐδέ με πείσεις.
ἦ ἐθέλεις, ὄφρ' αὐτὸς ἔχῃς γέρας, αὐτὰρ ἔμ' αὔτως
ἧσθαι δευόμενον, κέλεαι δέ με τήνδ' ἀποδοῦναι;
ἀλλ' εἰ μὲν δώσουσι γέρας μεγάθυμοι Ἀχαιοί,
ἄρσαντες κατὰ θυμόν, ὅπως ἀντάξιον ἔσται·
εἰ δέ κε μὴ δώωσιν, ἐγὼ δέ κεν αὐτὸς ἕλωμαι
ἢ τεὸν ἢ Αἴαντος ἰὼν γέρας, ἢ 'Οδυσῆος
ἄξω ἑλών· ὁ δέ κεν κεχολώσεται ὅν κεν ἵκωμαι.
ἀλλ' ἤτοι μὲν ταῦτα μεταφρασόμεσθα καὶ αὖτις,
νῦν δ' ἄγε νῆα μέλαιναν ἐρύσσομεν εἰς ἅλα δῖαν,

For the people's ruin grieves me, and their safety warms my heart.
Only, hark! some other booty find me straightway. It were shame
That alone of the Argeians of my prize bereft I came.
Witness all, my given portion passes from my hand again."

Then replied to him Achilles stout of foot, the flower of men.
"O Atrides, O of mortals mightiest, most gain-loving too!
Can it be the bold Achaians are to guerdon thee anew?
For we hold no stock in common: all we gat from cities' sack
We divided; 'twere not seemly that the folk should bring it back.
Make no more ado; to Phœbus send the rosy maid away;
We, the sons of the Achaians threefold, fourfold, will repay,
When we storm Troy's well-built bulwarks, if but Zeus shall bring the day!"

Answered sovran Agamemnon. "Think not, godlike Achilles,
Howsoever bold, to dupe us with devices such as these.
Neither shalt thou, cozening, foil me, neither bend. What prize is thine,
That thou keepest, but wilt have me, giving over what is mine,
Sit me down to lack my portion. Well; the maid I will resign
If the lofty-souled Achaians will another guerdon choose,
To my taste, of equal value. But, should they my word refuse,
What if I myself thy booty, or of Aias, go and take,
Or Odysseus? Whom I light on, into anger he will break.
But of this enough hereafter. Now upon the glorious main

ἐς δ' ἐρέτας ἐπιτηδὲς ἀγείρομεν, ἐς δ' ἑκατόμβην
θείομεν, ἂν δ' αὐτὴν Χρυσηΐδα καλλιπάρῃον
βήσομεν· εἷς δέ τις ἀρχὸς ἀνὴρ βουληφόρος ἔστω,
ἢ Αἴας, ἢ Ἰδομενεύς, ἢ δῖος Ὀδυσσεύς,
ἠὲ σύ, Πηλεΐδη, πάντων ἐκπαγλότατ' ἀνδρῶν,
ὄφρ' ἡμῖν ἑκάεργον ἱλάσσεαι ἱερὰ ῥέξας."
Τὸν δ' ἄρ' ὑπόδρα ἰδὼν προσέφη πόδας ὠκὺς Ἀχιλλεύς
"ὤμοι, ἀναιδείην ἐπιειμένε, κερδαλεόφρον,
πῶς τίς τοι πρόφρων ἔπεσιν πείθηται Ἀχαιῶν
ἢ ὁδὸν ἐλθέμεναι, ἢ ἀνδράσιν ἶφι μάχεσθαι;
οὐ γὰρ ἐγὼ Τρώων ἕνεκ' ἤλυθον αἰχμητάων
δεῦρο μαχησόμενος, ἐπεὶ οὔτι μοι αἴτιοί εἰσιν.
οὐ γὰρ πώποτ' ἐμὰς βοῦς ἤλασαν, οὐδὲ μὲν ἵππους,
οὐδέ ποτ' ἐν Φθίῃ ἐριβώλακι βωτιανείρῃ
καρπὸν ἐδηλήσαντ', ἐπειὴ μάλα πολλὰ μεταξὺ
οὔρεά τε σκιόεντα θάλασσά τε ἠχήεσσα·
ἀλλὰ σοί, ὦ μέγ' ἀναιδές, ἅμ' ἑσπόμεθ', ὄφρα σὺ χαίρῃς,
τιμὴν ἀρνύμενοι Μενελάῳ σοί τε, κυνῶπα,
πρὸς Τρώων· τῶν οὔτι μετατρέπῃ οὐδ' ἀλεγίζεις·
καὶ δή μοι γέρας αὐτὸς ἀφαιρήσεσθαι ἀπειλεῖς,
ᾧ ἔπι πολλ' ἐμόγησα, δόσαν δέ μοι υἷες Ἀχαιῶν.
οὐ μὲν σοί ποτε ἶσον ἔχω γέρας, ὁππότ' Ἀχαιοὶ
Τρώων ἐκπέρσωσ' εὐναιόμενον πτολίεθρον·
ἀλλὰ τὸ μὲν πλεῖον πολυάϊκος πολέμοιο
χεῖρες ἐμαὶ διέπουσ'· ἀτὰρ ἤν ποτε δασμὸς ἵκηται,

:h we straight a sable galley, and appoint a chosen train;
e hecatomb aboard, and let the rosy maid be ta'en
Chryseis; and for captain some one of our Council call,
domeneus, or Aias, or Odysseus, flower of all;
yself, most dread of mortals, son of Peleus, pass the seas,
for us thine holy offering Hecaergos may appease."
n with aspect stern addressing spake Achilles, swift of foot.
ıou, armed with shameless forehead, and with greed of gain to boot!
shall an Achaian chieftain willing follow thy command
r from afar to travel, or to lift in fight the hand?
not, No! the Trojan warriors brought me here in war to strive:
not I they harmed; my horses, oxen mine, they did not drive;
n the deep lands of Phthia, teeming nurse of heroes' pride,
d they my golden harvest; no, for, us from them to hide,
between the shadowy mountains, spread the sounding waters wide.
s thee, thou greatly shameless, thee, with doglike face, to please,
to serve and Menelaos that we followed o'er the seas,
ing honour from the Trojans for you twain. Thou giv'st no heed,
cest not, for this: but threatenest with thy hand to seize the meed
ed by the bold Achaians, earned by many a toilsome deed.
soever the Achaians sack some peopled city fair,
gathered Trojan booty, matched with thine, how small my share!
many-rushing battle, most, I ween, these hands dispatch;

σοὶ τὸ γέρας πολὺ μεῖζον, ἐγὼ δ' ὀλίγον τε φίλον τε
ἔρχομ' ἔχων ἐπὶ νῆας, ἐπὴν κεκάμω πολεμίζων.
νῦν δ' εἶμι Φθίηνδ', ἐπεὶ ἦ πολὺ φέρτερόν ἐστιν
οἴκαδ' ἴμεν σὺν νηυσὶ κορωνίσιν, οὐδέ σ' ὀΐω
ἐνθάδ' ἄτιμος ἐὼν ἄφενος καὶ πλοῦτον ἀφύξειν."
Τὸν δ' ἠμείβετ' ἔπειτα ἄναξ ἀνδρῶν Ἀγαμέμνων
"φεῦγε μάλ', εἴ τοι θυμὸς ἐπέσσυται, οὐδέ σ' ἔγωγε
λίσσομαι εἵνεκ' ἐμεῖο μένειν· πάρ' ἔμοιγε καὶ ἄλλοι
οἵ κέ με τιμήσουσι, μάλιστα δὲ μητιέτα Ζεύς.
ἔχθιστος δέ μοί ἐσσι διοτρεφέων βασιλήων·
αἰεὶ γάρ τοι ἔρις τε φίλη πόλεμοί τε μάχαι τε.
εἰ μάλα καρτερός ἐσσι, θεός που σοὶ τόγ' ἔδωκεν.
οἴκαδ' ἰὼν σὺν νηυσί τε σῇς καὶ σοῖς ἑτάροισι
Μυρμιδόνεσσιν ἄνασσε, σέθεν δ' ἐγὼ οὐκ ἀλεγίζω,
οὐδ' ὄθομαι κοτέοντος· ἀπειλήσω δέ τοι ὧδε·
ὡς ἔμ' ἀφαιρεῖται Χρυσηΐδα Φοῖβος Ἀπόλλων.
τὴν μὲν ἐγὼ σὺν νηΐ τ' ἐμῇ καὶ ἐμοῖς ἑτάροισι
πέμψω, ἐγὼ δέ κ' ἄγω Βρισηΐδα καλλιπάρῃον
αὐτὸς ἰὼν κλισίηνδε, τὸ σὸν γέρας, ὄφρ' εὖ εἰδῇς
ὅσσον φέρτερός εἰμι σέθεν, στυγέῃ δὲ καὶ ἄλλος
ἶσον ἐμοὶ φάσθαι καὶ ὁμοιωθήμεναι ἄντην."
Ὣς φάτο· Πηλεΐωνι δ' ἄχος γένετ', ἐν δέ οἱ ἦτορ
στήθεσσιν λασίοισι διάνδιχα μερμήριξεν,
ἢ ὅγε φάσγανον ὀξὺ ἐρυσσάμενος παρὰ μηροῦ
τοὺς μὲν ἀναστήσειεν, ὁ δ' Ἀτρεΐδην ἐναρίζοι,

Yet when distribution cometh, thine a plenteous prize to snatch,
Mine with scanty boon, yet cherished, to my galleys to retreat,
All war-wearied. Now, to Phthia. Better, with my beakèd fleet,
Better far, to journey homeward: neither brook I here to be,
Ill-entreated, void of honour, heaping goods and wealth for thee."
  Agamemnon, lord of heroes, straightway spake, "Thou say'st aright:
Flee, and welcome, if thy spirit urges thee to take to flight.
'Tis not I would pray thee linger, nor for cause of mine to fight.
Others here will pay me honour; most on Zeus all-wise I call.
Of the kings whom he hath nurtured, thee I fiercest hate of all;
Thy delight is still in wrangling, and in battle and in brawl.
If in might thou far surpassest, yet 'tis God that gave thee might.
With thy ships and with thy comrades homeward then take thou thy flight,
O'er the myrmidons to lord it: less than nought for thee I care,
Less than nought esteem thy anger; yet I give thee charge, beware:
Since the god Apollo Phœbus fair Chryseis doth demand,
With my ship, and with my comrades shall she go; but this my hand
From thy camp shall fetch Briseis, rosy-cheeked, thy guerdon dear,
That thou know me for thy better, and that others too may fear
Or to vie with me in honour, or to hold me for their peer."
  So he spake. Grief stung Pelīon; two-fold thoughts his mind divide:
Shall he draw the sharp-edged falchion, thrust the standers-by aside,
And rush on to slay Atrides; or within his shaggy breast

ἠὲ χόλον παύσειεν ἐρητύσειέ τε θυμόν.
ἕως ὁ ταῦθ' ὥρμαινε κατὰ φρένα καὶ κατὰ θυμὸν,
ἕλκετο δ' ἐκ κολεοῖο μέγα ξίφος, ἦλθε δ' Ἀθήνη
οὐρανόθεν· πρὸ γὰρ ἧκε θεὰ λευκώλενος Ἥρη,
ἄμφω ὁμῶς θυμῷ φιλέουσά τε κηδομένη τε.
στῆ δ' ὄπιθεν, ξανθῆς δὲ κόμης ἕλε Πηλείωνα,
οἴῳ φαινομένη· τῶν δ' ἄλλων οὔτις ὁρᾶτο.
θάμβησεν δ' Ἀχιλεὺς, μετὰ δ' ἐτράπετ', αὐτίκα δ' ἔγνω
Παλλάδ' Ἀθηναίην· δεινὼ δέ οἱ ὄσσε φάανθεν.
καί μιν φωνήσας ἔπεα πτερόεντα προσηύδα
  "Τίπτ' αὖτ', αἰγιόχοιο Διὸς τέκος, εἰλήλουθας;
ἦ ἵνα ὕβριν ἴδῃ Ἀγαμέμνονος Ἀτρείδαο;
ἀλλ' ἔκ τοι ἐρέω, τὸ δὲ καὶ τελέεσθαι ὀΐω·
ᾗς ὑπεροπλίῃσι τάχ' ἄν ποτε θυμὸν ὀλέσσῃ."
  Τὸν δ' αὖτε προσέειπε θεὰ γλαυκῶπις Ἀθήνη
"ἦλθον ἐγὼ παύσουσα τὸ σὸν μένος, αἴ κε πίθηαι,
οὐρανόθεν· πρὸ δέ μ' ἧκε θεὰ λευκώλενος Ἥρη,
ἄμφω ὁμῶς θυμῷ φιλέουσά τε κηδομένη τε.
ἀλλ' ἄγε, λῆγ' ἔριδος, μηδὲ ξίφος ἕλκεο χειρί·
ἀλλ' ἤτοι ἔπεσιν μὲν ὀνείδισον ὡς ἔσεταί περ.
ὧδε γὰρ ἐξερέω, τὸ δὲ καὶ τετελεσμένον ἔσται·
καί ποτέ τοι τρὶς τόσσα παρέσσεται ἄγλαα δῶρα
ὕβριος εἵνεκα τῆσδε· σὺ δ' ἴσχεο, πείθεο δ' ἡμῖν."
  Τὴν δ' ἀπαμειβόμενος προσέφη πόδας ὠκὺς Ἀχιλλεύς·
"χρὴ μὲν σφωΐτερόν γε, θεὰ, ἔπος εἰρύσσασθαι,

Shall he stay the kindled anger, and the fitful mood arrest?
While in mind and heart reflecting still he pondered on his doubt,
Yet his hand the mighty weapon from its sheath was drawing out.
Sent by Herè, white-armed goddess, then Athenè came from heaven;
Herè, who to both the chieftains equal care and love had given.
Near she stood behind Pelĭon, grasped him by his auburn hair;
Only for himself the vision, none beside him saw her there.
In surprise the hero turned him; there with awful eyes confest
Stood the goddess; and Achilles her in winged words addrest.

"Child of Zeus, the Ægis-bearer, wherefore art thou come? To see
Outrage done me by Atrides? more I say, and more shall be.
Insolence like his will haply bring with speed his day of doom."

Him the flashing-eyed Athenè straightway answered. "I am come,
If thou wilt, to stay thine anger; Herè sent me down from heaven;
Herè, who to both the chieftains equal love and care has given.
Come, let be thy giddy quarrel; draw not with thy hand the sword;
For the time, be words thy weapons; they in plenty shall be poured.
Since, in solemn speech that fails not, I foretell shall come the day
Thrice as much, of gifts as glorious thee, Achilles, shall repay
For this outrage done thine honour. Only curb thee, and obey."

Answered her the swift Achilles, "Meet it is to keep the word,
That ye twain enjoin, albeit wrath within be deeply stirred.

καὶ μάλα περ θυμῷ κεχολωμένον· ὣς γὰρ ἄμεινον.
ὅς κε θεοῖς ἐπιπείθηται, μάλα τ' ἔκλυον αὐτοῦ."
Ἦ, καὶ ἐπ' ἀργυρέῃ κώπῃ σχέθε χεῖρα βαρεῖαν,
ἂψ δ' ἐς κουλεὸν ὦσε μέγα ξίφος, οὐδ' ἀπίθησε
μύθῳ Ἀθηναίης· ἡ δ' Οὔλυμπόνδε βεβήκει
δώματ' ἐς αἰγιόχοιο Διὸς μετὰ δαίμονας ἄλλους.
Πηλείδης δ' ἐξαῦτις ἀταρτηροῖς ἐπέεσσιν
Ἀτρείδην προσέειπε, καὶ οὔπω λῆγε χόλοιο·
"Οἰνοβαρές, κυνὸς ὄμματ' ἔχων, κραδίην δ' ἐλάφοιο,
οὔτε ποτ' ἐς πόλεμον ἅμα λαῷ θωρηχθῆναι
οὔτε λόχονδ' ἰέναι σὺν ἀριστήεσσιν Ἀχαιῶν
τέτληκας θυμῷ· τὸ δέ τοι κὴρ εἴδεται εἶναι.
ἦ πολὺ λώϊόν ἐστι κατὰ στρατὸν εὐρὺν Ἀχαιῶν
δῶρ' ἀποαιρεῖσθαι, ὅστις σέθεν ἀντίον εἴπῃ.
δημοβόρος βασιλεύς, ἐπεὶ οὐτιδανοῖσιν ἀνάσσεις·
ἦ γὰρ ἄν, Ἀτρείδη, νῦν ὕστατα λωβήσαιο.
ἀλλ' ἔκ τοι ἐρέω καὶ ἐπὶ μέγαν ὅρκον ὀμοῦμαι·
ναὶ μὰ τόδε σκῆπτρον, τὸ μὲν οὔποτε φύλλα καὶ ὄζους
φύσει, ἐπειδὴ πρῶτα τομὴν ἐν ὄρεσσι λέλοιπεν,
οὐδ' ἀναθηλήσει· περὶ γάρ ῥά ἑ χαλκὸς ἔλεψεν
φύλλα τε καὶ φλοιόν· νῦν αὖτέ μιν υἷες Ἀχαιῶν
ἐν παλάμῃς φορέουσι δικασπόλοι, οἵτε θέμιστας
πρὸς Διὸς εἰρύαται· ὁ δέ τοι μέγας ἔσσεται ὅρκος·
ἦ ποτ' Ἀχιλλῆος ποθὴ ἵξεται υἷας Ἀχαιῶν
σύμπαντας· τότε δ' οὔτι δυνήσεαι ἀχνύμενός περ

Better so; the gods of heaven hear the man that them has heard."

Then upon the hilt of silver rested he his massive hand,
And again within the scabbard thrust he back the mighty brand.
Docile to the word of Pallas. She to her Olympian throne,
And the Ægis-bearer's mansions, and the gods, her peers, had gone.

Instantly the son of Peleus Agamemnon thus addrest,
Dark in speech and mischief-brooding; neither gave his passion rest.

"Wine-beladen son of Atreus! face of hound, and heart of deer!
Never hath thy spirit moved thee in the field to grasp the spear
With the troops, nor with the chieftains watch and wait in ambush drear.
Well thou know'st it. Sooth, 'tis better far, to plunder of his gifts
Whosoever in the army thwarting thee his voice uplifts.
Folk-devouring king! for surely mean are they that own thy sway;
Were they other, O Atrides, thou would'st sin thy last to day.
Yet a word shall now be spoken, and a mighty oath be sworn.
By the sceptre that I brandish, that nor twig nor leaf hath borne,
Since the time when on the mountains from its parent stem 'twas torn,
Nor shall bear, since bark and foliage all around the knife hath shorn—
Now the sons of the Achaians, set by Zeus to guard the right,
Bear it on the seat of judgment— will I swear an oath of might.
Time shall be, that for Achilles one and all the host shall long,

χραισμεῖν, εὖτ' ἂν πολλοὶ ὑφ' Ἕκτορος ἀνδροφόνοιο
θνήσκοντες πίπτωσι· σὺ δ' ἔνδοθι θυμὸν ἀμύξεις
χωόμενος, ὅτ' ἄριστον Ἀχαιῶν οὐδὲν ἔτισας."
  Ὣς φάτο Πηλείδης, ποτὶ δὲ σκῆπτρον βάλε γαίῃ
χρυσείοις ἥλοισι πεπαρμένον, ἕζετο δ' αὐτός·
Ἀτρείδης δ' ἑτέρωθεν ἐμήνιε. τοῖσι δὲΝέστ ωρ
ἡδυεπὴς ἀνόρουσε, λιγὺς Πυλίων ἀγορητής,
τοῦ καὶ ἀπὸ γλώσσης μέλιτος γλυκίων ῥέεν αὐδή
τῷ δ' ἤδη δύο μὲν γενεαὶ μερόπων ἀνθρώπων
ἐφθίαθ', οἵ οἱ πρόσθεν ἅμα τράφεν ἠδ' ἐγένοντο
ἐν Πύλῳ ἠγαθέῃ, μετὰ δὲ τριτάτοισιν ἄνασσεν—
ὅ σφιν ἐϋφρονέων ἀγορήσατο καὶ μετέειπεν
  "Ὢ πόποι, ἦ μέγα πένθος Ἀχαιΐδα γαῖαν ἱκάνει.
ἦ κεν γηθήσαι Πρίαμος Πριάμοιό τε παῖδες,
ἄλλοι τε Τρῶες μέγα κεν κεχαροίατο θυμῷ,
εἰ σφῶϊν τάδε πάντα πυθοίατο μαρναμένοιιν,
οἳ περὶ μὲν βουλὴν Δαναῶν, περὶ δ' ἐστὲ μάχεσθαι.
ἀλλὰ πίθεσθ'· ἄμφω δὲ νεωτέρω ἐστὸν ἐμεῖο.
ἤδη γάρ ποτ' ἐγὼ καὶ ἀρείοσιν ἠέπερ ὑμῖν
ἀνδράσιν ὡμίλησα, καὶ οὔποτέ μ' οἵγ' ἀθέριζον.
οὐ γάρ πω τοίους ἴδον ἀνέρας οὐδὲ ἴδωμαι,
οἷον Πειρίθοόν τε Δρύαντά τε, ποιμένα λαῶν,
Καινέα τ' Ἐξάδιόν τε καὶ ἀντίθεον Πολύφημον
[Θησέα τ' Αἰγείδην, ἐπιείκελον ἀθανάτοισιν].
κάρτιστοι δὴ κεῖνοι ἐπιχθονίων τράφεν ἀνδρῶν·

When the hand of murderous Hector fells to earth a dying throng;
Vain thy grief to aid them; skulking thou shalt tear with rage thy breast,
That of all the bold Achaians thou didst put to shame the best."

So Pelides. And his sceptre, golden-studded, down he flung;
Then he sate. Nor less Atrides raging fumed. Up Nestor sprung
Fluent orator of Pylos gentle-worded; from his tongue
Melted tones than honey sweeter; there had passed within his day,
Speaking men, in goodly Pylos generations twain away;
He amidst the third was ruling. Such he spake, a friend to friends.

"Gods in heaven! why what sorrow o'er Achaiis now impends!
Truly Priam, and his children, and all Troy would take delight,
Were they once to learn the tidings that ye twain thus fiercely fight;
Ye, the first in arms of Danaans, and the first in council too.
Be persuaded. Ye are younger, both, than I; who had to do
(Nor did they at least despise me,) e'en with better men than you.
Never heretofore I saw, nor e'er shall see the match again
Of Pirithoos, and Druas like a shepherd ruling men,
Of Exadios and Kaineus; Poluphemos, that might vie
With Immortals; Ægid Theseus, image of the gods on high.
These the mightiest were of mortals; with the mightiest they fought,

κάρτιστοι μὲν ἔσαν καὶ καρτίστοις ἐμάχοντο,
φηρσὶν ὀρεσκῴοισι, καὶ ἐκπάγλως ἀπόλεσσαν.
καὶ μὲν τοῖσιν ἐγὼ μεθομίλεον ἐκ Πύλου ἐλθών,
τηλόθεν ἐξ ἀπίης γαίης· καλέσαντο γὰρ αὐτοί·
καὶ μαχόμην κατ' ἔμ' αὐτὸν ἐγώ· κείνοισι δ' ἂν οὔτις
τῶν οἳ νῦν βροτοί εἰσιν ἐπιχθόνιοι μαχέοιτο.
καὶ μέν μευ βουλέων ξύνιεν πείθοντό τε μύθῳ.
ἀλλὰ πίθεσθε καὶ ὔμμες, ἐπεὶ πείθεσθαι ἄμεινον.
μήτε σὺ τόνδ', ἀγαθός περ ἐών, ἀποαίρεο κούρην,
ἀλλ' ἔα, ὥς οἱ πρῶτα δόσαν γέρας υἷες Ἀχαιῶν·
μήτε σύ, Πηλείδη, θέλ' ἐριζέμεναι βασιλῆϊ
ἀντιβίην, ἐπεὶ οὔποθ' ὁμοίης ἔμμορε τιμῆς
σκηπτοῦχος βασιλεύς, ᾧτε Ζεὺς κῦδος ἔδωκεν.
εἰ δὲ σὺ κάρτερος ἐσσι, θεὰ δέ σε γείνατο μήτηρ,
ἀλλ' ὅγε φέρτερός ἐστιν, ἐπεὶ πλεόνεσσιν ἀνάσσει.
Ἀτρείδη, σὺ δὲ παῦε τεὸν μένος· αὐτὰρ ἔγωγε
λίσσομ' Ἀχιλλῆϊ μεθέμεν χόλον, ὃς μέγα πᾶσιν
ἕρκος Ἀχαιοῖσιν πέλεται πολέμοιο κακοῖο."

Τὸν δ' ἀπαμειβόμενος προσέφη κρείων Ἀγαμέμνων
" ναὶ δὴ ταῦτά γε πάντα, γέρον, κατὰ μοῖραν ἔειπες.
ἀλλ' ὅδ' ἀνὴρ ἐθέλει περὶ πάντων ἔμμεναι ἄλλων,
πάντων μὲν κρατέειν ἐθέλει, πάντεσσι δ' ἀνάσσειν,
πᾶσι δὲ σημαίνειν, ἅ τιν' οὐ πείσεσθαι ὀΐω.
εἰ δέ μιν αἰχμητὴν ἔθεσαν θεοὶ αἰὲν ἐόντες,
τοὔνεκά οἱ προθέουσιν ὀνείδεα μυθήσασθαι;"

With the mountain-haunting Centaurs, and to mighty ruin brought.
'Twas with these I mixed; from Pylos coming, distant Apian land.
They had called me. In the combat I, too, wielded then the brand.
Them no mortal now surviving for a moment would withstand.
They could hearken to my counsel, yielded they to my discourse;
Ye then also be persuaded: better reason is than force.
Thou, Atrides, though so potent, take the damsel not away:
As the sons of the Achaians gave her first, so let her stay.
Thou, Pelides, be not forward thus to quarrel with the King;
Zeus to sceptred kings gave glory, none can equal honours bring.
And, if thou art stout and valiant, and a goddess gave thee birth,
Yet is he thy better, ruling wider over men on earth.
Calm thy spirit then, Atrides: and thy wrath—'tis I who pray—
Yield, Achilles, best of bulwarks in the deadly battle fray."

Answered him Atrides. "Truly all thou say'st is right well said:
But, old friend, this man endeavours o'er the world to lift his head;
On us all to put the bridle, o'er us all the lord to play,
Of us all to be commander: claims like these, I say them nay.
If the gods that live for ever granted him the warrior's part,
Not for this they lent him warrant that his tongue should venom dart."

Τὸν δ' ἄρ' ὑποβλήδην ἠμείβετο δῖος 'Αχιλλεύς
" ἦ γάρ κεν δειλός τε καὶ οὐτιδανὸς καλεοίμην,
εἰ δὴ σοὶ πᾶν ἔργον ὑπείξομαι, ὅττι κεν εἴπῃς·
ἄλλοισιν δὴ ταῦτ' ἐπιτέλλεο, μὴ γὰρ ἔμοιγε
[σήμαιν'· οὐ γὰρ ἔγωγ' ἔτι σοι πείσεσθαι ὀΐω].
ἄλλο δέ τοι ἐρέω, σὺ δ' ἐνὶ φρεσὶ βάλλεο σῇσιν·
χερσὶ μὲν οὔτοι ἔγωγε μαχήσομαι εἵνεκα κούρης
οὔτε σοὶ οὔτε τῳ ἄλλῳ, ἐπεί μ' ἀφέλεσθέ γε δόντες·
τῶν δ' ἄλλων ἅ μοί ἐστι θοῇ παρὰ νηῒ μελαίνῃ,
τῶν οὐκ ἄν τι φέροις ἀνελὼν ἀέκοντος ἐμεῖο.
εἰ δ' ἄγε μήν, πείρησαι, ἵνα γνώωσι καὶ οἵδε·
αἶψά τοι αἷμα κελαινὸν ἐρωήσει περὶ δουρί."
"Ὣς τώγ' ἀντιβίοισι μαχησαμένω ἐπέεσσιν
ἀνστήτην, λῦσαν δ' ἀγορὴν παρὰ νηυσὶν 'Αχαιῶν.
Πηλείδης μὲν ἐπὶ κλισίας καὶ νῆας ἐΐσας
ἤϊε σύν τε Μενοιτιάδῃ καὶ οἷς ἑτάροισιν·
'Ατρείδης δ' ἄρα νῆα θοὴν ἅλαδε προέρυσσεν,
ἐς δ' ἐρέτας ἔκρινεν ἐείκοσιν, ἐς δ' ἑκατόμβην
βῆσε θεῷ, ἀνὰ δὲ Χρυσηΐδα καλλιπάρῃον
εἷσεν ἄγων· ἐν δ' ἀρχὸς ἔβη πολύμητις 'Οδυσσεύς.
Οἱ μὲν ἔπειτ' ἀναβάντες ἐπέπλεον ὑγρὰ κέλευθα,
λαοὺς δ' 'Ατρείδης ἀπολυμαίνεσθαι ἄνωγεν.
οἱ δ' ἀπελυμαίνοντο καὶ εἰς ἅλα λύματ' ἔβαλλον,
ἔρδον δ' 'Απόλλωνι τεληέσσας ἑκατόμβας
ταύρων ἠδ' αἰγῶν παρὰ θῖν' ἁλὸς ἀτρυγέτοιο·

Brake upon the king Achilles, flower of men, in swift reply.
"Call me craven, for thou may'st it, yea the name of man deny,
When I yield thee all thou listest. No, let baser men obey:
Think not to be my commander; henceforth I disown thy sway.
More I tell thee, and I bid thee be it pondered while it may.
For the damsel that ye gave me, since ye now take back the gift,
Nor with thee to fight, nor other, this my hand I will not lift.
But, beside my dark swift galley whatsoever resteth still,
O I warn thee, Agamemnon, touch not aught against my will.
Nay, go try it, if thou willest, so that all may know, who hear;
Soon thy spurting blood shall darken, with its purple flow, my spear."

So they two, in speech still battling, each the other fierce opposed;
By the ships of the Achaians then the great Assembly closed.
With Patroclos and his comrades, to his camp and well-trimmed ships
Went Pelides. But Atrides straight a fleetest bark equips;
With an hecatomb 'tis laden, with a score of rowers manned,
And he leads the rosy maiden, to the vessel from the strand,
And Odysseus, rich in counsel, is the captain of the band.

They departing made their voyage o'er the furrows of the main;
But Atrides bade purgation, that the folk might heal again.
Then the people dipped, and seaward duly cast away the stain.
Next, beside the main untrampled, spotless and in number full,
Offered they to great Apollo, hecatomb of goat and bull.

κνίση δ' οὐρανὸν ἶκεν ἑλισσομένη περὶ καπνῷ.
῞Ως οἱ μὲν τὰ πένοντο κατὰ στρατόν· οὐδ' Ἀγαμέμνων
λῆγ' ἔριδος, τὴν πρῶτον ἐπηπείλησ' Ἀχιλῆϊ,
ἀλλ' ὅγε Ταλθύβιόν τε καὶ Εὐρυβάτην προσέειπεν,
τώ οἱ ἔσαν κήρυκε καὶ ὀτρηρὼ θεράποντε·
"Ἔρχεσθον κλισίην Πηληϊάδεω Ἀχιλῆος·
χειρὸς ἑλόντ' ἀγέμεν Βρισηΐδα καλλιπάρηον·
εἰ δέ κε μὴ δώησιν, ἐγὼ δέ κεν αὐτὸς ἕλωμαι
ἐλθὼν σὺν πλεόνεσσι· τό οἱ καὶ ῥίγιον ἔσται."
῞Ως εἰπὼν προΐει, κρατερὸν δ' ἐπὶ μῦθον ἔτελλεν.
τὼ δ' ἀέκοντε βατην παρὰ θῖν' ἁλὸς ἀτρυγέτοιο,
Μυρμιδόνων δ' ἐπί τε κλισίας καὶ νῆας ἱκέσθην.
τὸν δ' εὗρον παρά τε κλισίῃ καὶ νηῒ μελαίνῃ
ἥμενον· οὐδ' ἄρα τώγε ἰδὼν γήθησεν Ἀχιλλεύς.
τὼ μὲν ταρβήσαντε καὶ αἰδομένω βασιλῆα
στήτην, οὐδέ τί μιν προσεφώνεον οὐδ' ἐρέοντο·
αὐτὰρ ὁ ἔγνω ᾗσιν ἐνὶ φρεσί, φώνησέν τε
"Χαίρετε, κήρυκες, Διὸς ἄγγελοι ἠδὲ καὶ ἀνδρῶν,
ἆσσον ἴτ'· οὔτι μοι ὔμμες ἐπαίτιοι, ἀλλ' Ἀγαμέμνων,
ὃ σφῶϊ προΐει Βρισηΐδος εἵνεκα κούρης.
ἀλλ' ἄγε, Διογενὲς Πατρόκλεις, ἔξαγε κούρην
καί σφωιν δὸς ἄγειν. τὼ δ' αὐτὼ μάρτυροι ἔστων
πρός τε θεῶν μακάρων πρός τε θνητῶν ἀνθρώπων
καὶ πρὸς τοῦ βασιλῆος ἀπηνέος, εἴποτε δ' αὖτε
χρειὼ ἐμεῖο γένηται ἀεικέα λοιγὸν ἀμῦναι

With the curling smoke, the savour high as heaven ascending went.

Such their cares within the camp. But Agamemnon, sternly bent
On the strife that he had threatened, straightway good Talthubios sent
And Eurybates; his heralds, and his trusty squires, were they.

"To the barrack of Achilles, son of Peleus, wend your way;
Bring the rosy maid Briseis by the hand; if he refuse,
And compel me to go fetch her with a following—let him choose."

Thus he spake; and so dismissed them, charged with words of harsh disdain.
They reluctant paced the margin of the free untrampled main,
To the Myrmidon encampment. Near his ship, and by his door
Sate Pelides. As he saw them, little joy his aspect wore.
Trembling they revered the king, and silent stood, as men distraught;
But Achilles straight addressed them, well discerning all their thought.

"Heralds, hail! not men's alone, but Zeus's Envoys: fear ye nought:
You I blame not. On Atrides all the load of wrong be laid:
Ye are come to take Briseis; Prince Patroclos, fetch the maid;
Give her; take her. Yet, O heralds! witnesses you twain I bring,
In the name of gods and mortals, aye, and of that ruthless King,
If he henceforth can require me in his need and darkest day
From the host of the Argeians shameful scathe to ward away!

τοῖς ἄλλοις. ἦ γὰρ ὅγ' ὀλοιῇσι φρεσὶ θύει,
οὐδέ τι οἶδε νοῆσαι ἅμα πρόσσω καὶ ὀπίσσω,
ὅππως οἱ παρὰ νηυσὶ σόοι μαχέοιντο Ἀχαιοί."
Ὣς φάτο, Πάτροκλος δὲ φίλῳ ἐπεπείθεθ' ἑταίρῳ,
ἐκ δ' ἄγαγε κλισίης Βρισηΐδα καλλιπάρῃον,
δῶκε δ' ἄγειν· τὼ δ' αὖτις ἴτην παρὰ νῆας Ἀχαιῶν·
ἡ δ' ἀέκουσ' ἅμα τοῖσι γυνὴ κίεν. αὐτὰρ Ἀχιλλεὺς
δακρύσας ἑτάρων ἄφαρ ἕζετο νόσφι λιασθεὶς,
θῖν' ἔφ' ἁλὸς πολιῆς, ὁρόων ἐπ' ἀπείρονα πόντον·
πολλὰ δὲ μητρὶ φίλῃ ἠρήσατο χεῖρας ὀρεγνύς·
"Μῆτερ, ἐπεί μ' ἔτεκές γε μινυνθάδιόν περ ἐόντα,
τιμήν πέρ μοι ὄφελλεν Ὀλύμπιος ἐγγυαλίξαι,
Ζεὺς ὑψιβρεμέτης· νῦν δ' οὐδέ με τυτθὸν ἔτισεν.
ἦ γάρ μ' Ἀτρείδης εὐρυκρείων Ἀγαμέμνων
ἠτίμησεν· ἑλὼν γὰρ ἔχει γέρας, αὐτὸς ἀπούρας."
Ὣς φάτο δακρυχέων, τοῦ δ' ἔκλυε πότνια μήτηρ
ἡμένη ἐν βένθεσσιν ἁλὸς παρὰ πατρὶ γέροντι.
καρπαλίμως δ' ἀνέδυ πολιῆς ἁλὸς ἠΰτ' ὀμίχλη,
καί ῥα πάροιθ' αὐτοῖο καθέζετο δακρυχέοντος,
χειρί τέ μιν κατέρεξεν, ἔπος τ' ἔφατ' ἔκ τ' ὀνόμαζεν·
"Τέκνον, τί κλαίεις; τί δέ σε φρένας ἵκετο πένθος;
ἐξαύδα, μὴ κεῦθε νόῳ, ἵνα εἴδομεν ἄμφω."
Τὴν δὲ βαρυστενάχων προσέφη πόδας ὠκὺς Ἀχιλλεύς·
"οἶσθα· τίη τοι ταῦτα ἰδυίῃ πάντ' ἀγορεύω;
ᾠχόμεθ' ἐς Θήβην, ἱερὴν πόλιν Ἠετίωνος,

Passion-blinded King! he learns not what hath been, or what shall be,
That in safety his Achaians still may war beside the sea."

He had spoken; and Patroclos straight his comrade dear obeyed.
From the door he led, and gave them to conduct, the rosy maid.
For the camp the two departed. She with them unwilling goes.
But Achilles from his comrades sits afar, and weeps his woes,
Gazes o'er the purple waters, by the breakers on the strand,
And full often to his mother stretches forth in prayer his hand.

"Mother! for thou art my mother, though my destined years be few,
From the Thunderer Zeus Olympian surely honour was my due;
Yet he honours not, but shames me, for Atrides, wide of sway,
Hath disgraced me, and unpunished holds the prize he took away."

Heard him then his goddess mother, as with tears his grief he told,
Sitting in the salt abysses, by her sire, the sea-god old.
Straight she issued from the waters, like a vapour, to the strand,
Sate beside him as he wept, and gently soothed him with her hand,
And addressed him as her offspring. "Wherefore weep'st, what ail'st, my son?
Tell it, hide it not within thee, that we make our sorrows one."

Swift Achilles, deeply groaning, answered her, "Thou know'st full well.
Why to thee, aware already, should I tale of sorrow tell?
How we reached Eetion's city, sacred Thebe, burned it, bare

τὴν δὲ διεπράθομέν τε καὶ ἤγομεν ἐνθάδε πάντα.
καὶ τὰ μὲν εὖ δάσσαντο μετὰ σφίσιν υἷες Ἀχαιῶν,
ἐκ δ' ἕλον Ἀτρεΐδῃ Χρυσηΐδα καλλιπάρῃον.
Χρύσης δ' αὖθ', ἱερεὺς ἑκατηβόλου Ἀπόλλωνος,
ἦλθε θοὰς ἐπὶ νῆας Ἀχαιῶν χαλκοχιτώνων
λυσόμενός τε θύγατρα φέρων τ' ἀπερείσι' ἄποινα,
στέμματ' ἔχων ἐν χερσὶν ἑκηβόλου Ἀπόλλωνος
χρυσέῳ ἀνὰ σκήπτρῳ, καὶ ἐλίσσετο πάντας Ἀχαιούς,
Ἀτρεΐδα δὲ μάλιστα δύω, κοσμήτορε λαῶν.
ἔνθ' ἄλλοι μὲν πάντες ἐπευφήμησαν Ἀχαιοὶ
αἰδεῖσθαί θ' ἱερῆα καὶ ἀγλαὰ δέχθαι ἄποινα·
ἀλλ' οὐκ Ἀτρεΐδῃ Ἀγαμέμνονι ἥνδανε θυμῷ,
ἀλλὰ κακῶς ἀφίει, κρατερὸν δ' ἐπὶ μῦθον ἔτελλεν.
χωόμενος δ' ὁ γέρων πάλιν ᾤχετο· τοῖο δ' Ἀπόλλων
εὐξαμένου ἤκουσεν, ἐπεὶ μάλα οἱ φίλος ἦεν,
ἧκε δ' ἐπ' Ἀργείοισι κακὸν βέλος· οἱ δέ νυ λαοὶ
θνῆσκον ἐπασσύτεροι, τὰ δ' ἐπῴχετο κῆλα θεοῖο
πάντη ἀνὰ στρατὸν εὐρὺν Ἀχαιῶν. ἄμμι δὲ μάντις
εὖ εἰδὼς ἀγόρευε θεοπροπίας ἑκάτοιο.
αὐτίκ' ἐγὼ πρῶτος κελόμην θεὸν ἱλάσκεσθαι·
Ἀτρεΐωνα δ' ἔπειτα χόλος λάβεν, αἶψα δ' ἀναστὰς
ἠπείλησεν μῦθον, ὃ δὴ τετελεσμένος ἐστίν.
τὴν μὲν γὰρ σὺν νηῒ θοῇ ἑλίκωπες Ἀχαιοὶ
ἐς Χρύσην πέμπουσιν, ἄγουσι δὲ δῶρα ἄνακτι·
τὴν δὲ νέον κλισίηθεν ἔβαν κήρυκες ἄγοντες.

Hither all the spoil; reserving, as we took each man his share,
For Atrides first the rosy child of Chryses, maiden fair.
Then did he, the priest of Phœbus, darting shafts from far, repair
To the armour-clad Achaians at their ships, with presents rare,
For the ransom of his daughter. In his hand the garlands were
On the golden staff of Phœbus; Suppliant to the chiefs he spoke,
Most of all the two Atridai, the commanders of the folk.
Then Apollo's priest to honour all th' Achaians answered yea.
And to take the costly ransom; one, one only, said him nay,
And, with speech full rude and scornful, drave the ancient man away,
Agamemnon, son of Atreus. Back, in wrath, his wrong to tell,
Went the priestly sire. Apollo heard him, for he loved him well;
Then he shot the evil arrow, and the folk by thousands died;
O'er the host of the Achaians darts of heav'n were ranging wide.
Thereupon the Seer inspirèd told the mind of Hecatos:
I the first the Chiefs exhorted, 'Soothe the god, and stay the loss.'
Choler straight inflamed Atrides: quick he rose, and threatening spake
That which he hath since accomplished. Solemnly the maid they take,

κούρην Βρισῆος, τήν μοι δόσαν υἷες Ἀχαιῶν.
ἀλλὰ σύ, εἰ δύνασαί γε, περίσχεο παιδὸς ἑῆος·
ἐλθοῦσ᾽ Οὔλυμπόνδε Δία λίσαι, εἴποτε δή τι
ἢ ἔπει ὤνησας κραδίην Διὸς ἠὲ καὶ ἔργῳ.
πολλάκι γάρ σεο πατρὸς ἐνὶ μεγάροισιν ἄκουσα
εὐχομένης, ὅτ᾽ ἔφησθα κελαινεφέϊ Κρονίωνι
οἴη ἐν ἀθανάτοισιν ἀεικέα λοιγὸν ἀμῦναι,
ὁππότε μιν ξυνδῆσαι Ὀλύμπιοι ἤθελον ἄλλοι,
Ἥρη τ᾽ ἠδὲ Ποσειδάων καὶ Παλλὰς Ἀθήνη·
ἀλλὰ σὺ τόνγ᾽ ἐλθοῦσα, θεά, ὑπελύσαο δεσμῶν,
ὦχ᾽ ἑκατόγχειρον καλέσασ᾽ ἐς μακρὸν Ὄλυμπον,
ὃν Βριάρεων καλέουσι θεοί, ἄνδρες δέ τε πάντες
Αἰγαίων᾽—ὁ γὰρ αὖτε βίῃ οὗ πατρὸς ἀμείνων—
ὅς ῥα παρὰ Κρονίωνι καθέζετο κύδεϊ γαίων·
τὸν καὶ ὑπέδδεισαν μάκαρες θεοὶ οὐδέ τ᾽ ἔδησαν.
τῶν νῦν μιν μνήσασα παρέζεο καὶ λαβὲ γούνων,
αἴ κέν πως ἐθέλῃσιν ἐπὶ Τρώεσσιν ἀρῆξαι,
τοὺς δὲ κατὰ πρύμνας τε καὶ ἀμφ᾽ ἅλα ἔλσαι Ἀχαιοὺς
κτεινομένους, ἵνα πάντες ἐπαύρωνται βασιλῆος,
γνῷ δὲ καὶ Ἀτρεΐδης εὐρυκρείων Ἀγαμέμνων
ἣν ἄτην, ὅτ᾽ ἄριστον Ἀχαιῶν οὐδὲν ἔτισεν."
Τὸν δ᾽ ἠμείβετ᾽ ἔπειτα Θέτις κατὰ δάκρυ χέουσα
"ὤμοι, τέκνον ἐμόν, τί νύ σ᾽ ἔτρεφον αἰνὰ τεκοῦσα;
αἴθ᾽ ὄφελες παρὰ νηυσὶν ἀδάκρυτος καὶ ἀπήμων
ἧσθαι, ἐπεί νύ τοι αἶσα μίνυνθά περ, οὔτι μάλα δήν·

Flashing-eyed Achaians take her, while I speak it, o'er the foam,
With the offerings for Apollo, in the quick ship, to her home.
But the daughter fair of Brises, even now the heralds sped,
And the guerdon comrades gave me from my barrack they have led.
Mother! now, for thou art able, thine own warrior-son defend:
Mount Olympus; pray Kronion, if indeed by act or word
Thou hast ever done him service: for full oft mine ears have heard,
Heard thee proudly tell, when seated Queen within my Father's hall,
How, alone of the Immortals, thou didst save from shameful thrall
Zeus the cloud-wrapt. All Olympus fast to chain him had designed;
Poseidaon with Queen Herè and Athenè was combined;
But thou camest, as a goddess, to relieve him from his bands,
Swiftly fetching to Olympus him that bears the hundred hands,
Briareus immortals call him, and Aigaion men on earth:
He in vasty strength surpassing e'en the sire that gave him birth,
Sate him down beside Kronion, and exulted in his might;
Quailèd all the blessed gods, and changed their counsel, at the sight.
Go, sit near him, and remind him, and lay hold upon his knees,
If perchance his will may move him both to give the Trojans ease,
And in rout the Danaan army to the ships and strand to bring,
That the folk in blood and slaughter, may take pleasure in its King;
While wide-ruling Agamemnon may at length his sin detest,
That of all the bold Achaians he hath put to shame the best."

Him, in weeping, Thetis answered, "Ah, my son, what woe is me!
Wherefore did I rear thee upward, dreadful birth, why bore I thee?
Would that, since thy fate assigns thee but a little while to be,
Thou hadst rested by the vessels, tearless, and from outrage free.

νῦν δ' ἅμα τ' ὠκύμορος καὶ ὀϊζυρὸς περὶ πάντων
ἔπλεο· τῷ σε κακῇ αἴσῃ τέκον ἐν μεγάροισιν.
τοῦτο δέ τοι ἐρέουσα ἔπος Διὶ τερπικεραύνῳ
εἶμ' αὐτὴ πρὸς Ὄλυμπον ἀγάννιφον, αἴ κε πίθηται.
ἀλλὰ σὺ μὲν νῦν νηυσὶ παρήμενος ὠκυπόροισιν
μήνι' Ἀχαιοῖσιν, πολέμου δ' ἀποπαύεο πάμπαν·
Ζεὺς γὰρ ἐς Ὠκεανὸν μετ' ἀμύμονας Αἰθιοπῆας
χθιζὸς ἔβη κατὰ δαῖτα, θεοὶ δ' ἅμα πάντες ἕποντο·
δωδεκάτῃ δέ τοι αὖτις ἐλεύσεται Οὔλυμπόνδε,
καὶ τότ' ἔπειτά τοι εἶμι Διὸς ποτὶ χαλκοβατὲς δῶ,
καί μιν γουνάσομαι, καί μιν πείσεσθαι ὀΐω."
Ὣς ἄρα φωνήσασ' ἀπεβήσετο, τὸν δ' ἔλιπ' αὐτοῦ
χωόμενον κατὰ θυμὸν ἐϋζώνοιο γυναικὸς,
τήν ῥα βίῃ ἀέκοντος ἀπηύρων. αὐτὰρ Ὀδυσσεὺς
ἐς Χρύσην ἵκανεν ἄγων ἱερὴν ἑκατόμβην.
οἱ δ' ὅτε δὴ λιμένος πολυβενθέος ἐντὸς ἵκοντο,
ἱστία μὲν στείλαντο, θέσαν δ' ἐν νηῒ μελαίνῃ,
ἱστὸν δ' ἱστοδόκῃ πέλασαν προτόνοισιν ὑφέντες
καρπαλίμως, τὴν δ' εἰς ὅρμον προέρεσσαν ἐρετμοῖς.
ἐκ δ' εὐνὰς ἔβαλον, κατὰ δὲ πρυμνήσι' ἔδησαν·
ἐκ δὲ καὶ αὐτοὶ βαῖνον ἐπὶ ῥηγμῖνι θαλάσσης,
ἐκ δ' ἑκατόμβην βῆσαν ἑκηβόλῳ Ἀπόλλωνι·
ἐκ δὲ Χρυσηῒς νηὸς βῆ ποντοπόροιο.
τὴν μὲν ἔπειτ' ἐπὶ βωμὸν ἄγων πολύμητις Ὀδυσσεὺς
πατρὶ φίλῳ ἐν χερσὶ τίθει, καί μιν προσέειπεν

Now, thy lot, of all men mortal, shortest both and saddest falls;
Evil was the doom that made me bear thee in thy father's halls.
But I mount—for he may hearken— to Olympus wrapt in snow,
That to Zeus, whose sport is thunder, I may all thy bidding show.
Yet beside the winged vessels bide awhile; indulge thy rage
Toward the sons of the Achaians; and no more the battle wage.
For to Ocean and the Æthiops, noble race, went yesterday
Zeus with all the gods a-feasting. Suns eleven must pass away,
E'er again they reach Olympus. Then on Zeus's floor of brass
Will I stand, his knees embracing, and will bring thy thought to pass.

So she spake; and went. Indignant on his wrath he brooded still,
For the slender-waisted woman, whom they took despite his will.

But Odysseus came to Chryse, with the holy hecatomb,
Entered in the spacious harbour, furled the sails, and found them room
In the dark ship's hold; with halyards brought the tall mast heeling o'er
Briskly; then with strokes of vigour gave the vessel way ashore.
Forth they cast the solid anchors, and the stern-ropes tightly bound;
Forth they sprang upon the sea-beach, forth the hecatomb to ground
Brought they for the Archer Phœbus; forth Chryseis came to land
From the wave-borne ship. Odysseus rich in counsel, up the strand
Toward the altar led, and gave her safely to her father's hand.

"Ὦ Χρύση, πρό μ' ἔπεμψεν ἄναξ ἀνδρῶν Ἀγαμέμνων
παῖδά τε σοὶ ἀγέμεν, Φοίβῳ θ' ἱερὴν ἑκατόμβην
ῥέξαι ὑπὲρ Δαναῶν, ὄφρ' ἱλασόμεσθα ἄνακτα,
ὃς νῦν Ἀργείοισι πολύστονα κήδε' ἐφῆκεν."
Ὣς εἰπὼν ἐν χερσὶ τίθει, ὁ δ' ἐδέξατο χαίρων
παῖδα φίλην· τοὶ δ' ὦκα θεῷ κλειτὴν ἑκατόμβην
ἑξείης ἔστησαν ἐΰδμητον περὶ βωμόν,
χερνίψαντο δ' ἔπειτα καὶ οὐλοχύτας ἀνέλοντο.
τοῖσιν δὲ Χρύσης μεγάλ' εὔχετο χεῖρας ἀνασχών·
"Κλῦθί μευ, ἀργυρότοξ', ὃς Χρύσην ἀμφιβέβηκας
Κίλλαν τε ζαθέην, Τενέδοιό τε ἶφι ἀνάσσεις·
ἠμὲν δή ποτ' ἐμεῦ πάρος ἔκλυες εὐξαμένοιο,
τίμησας μὲν ἐμέ, μέγα δ' ἴψαο λαὸν Ἀχαιῶν·
ἠδ' ἔτι καὶ νῦν μοι τόδ' ἐπικρήηνον ἐέλδωρ·
ἤδη νῦν Δαναοῖσιν ἀεικέα λοιγὸν ἄμυνον."
Ὣς ἔφατ' εὐχόμενος, τοῦ δ' ἔκλυε Φοῖβος Ἀπόλλων.
αὐτὰρ ἐπεί ῥ' εὔξαντο καὶ οὐλοχύτας προβάλοντο,
αὖ ἔρυσαν μὲν πρῶτα καὶ ἔσφαξαν καὶ ἔδειραν,
μηρούς τ' ἐξέταμον κατά τε κνίσσῃ ἐκάλυψαν
δίπτυχα ποιήσαντες, ἐπ' αὐτῶν δ' ὠμοθέτησαν.
καῖε δ' ἐπὶ σχίζῃς ὁ γέρων, ἐπὶ δ' αἴθοπα οἶνον
λεῖβε· νέοι δὲ παρ' αὐτὸν ἔχον πεμπώβολα χερσίν.
αὐτὰρ ἐπεὶ κατὰ μῆρ' ἐκάη καὶ σπλάγχν' ἐπάσαντο,
μίστυλλόν τ' ἄρα τἆλλα καὶ ἀμφ' ὀβελοῖσιν ἔπειραν,
ὤπτησάν τε περιφραδέως, ἐρύσαντό τε πάντα.

"Agamemnon, lord of heroes bade me lead thy daughter home,
And, for sacrifice to Phœbus, bring the holy hecatomb,
Thus, O Chryses! for the Danaans that the god we may appease,
Him that now against th' Argeians sorrows numberless decrees.
So he spake; and to her father then delivered up the maid,
Who with joy received her. Quickly they the hecatomb arrayed
Round about the well-built altar; noble gift, to Phœbus paid.
Then they made the due ablution, waved the barley grains on high:
Chryses prayed aloud, and lifted both his hands toward the sky.
"Hear thou, silver-bowed Apollo, that in Chryse dost delight
And in holiest Killa, thou that rulest Tenedos with might!
As before thou heard'st me praying, and with honour didst me right,
And didst sorely hurt the Danaans; hear me once again to-day,
Yes, to-day from the Achaians shameful ruin ward away.
Thus he spake his vows: Apollo Phœbus heard him, as he prayed.
Ended then their supplications, and the barley sprinklings made,
First the necks they twisted backward, then they killed the beasts, and flayed;
Then cut out the thighs, and wrapt them each in fat with double coil,
Placing o'er them bits, for Chryses o'er the cloven logs to broil.
Glowing wine he poured upon them, as they broiled; a goodly band
Of the youths stood by assisting, with their five-prong forks in hand.
Thighs now burned, and entrails tasted, sliced and spitted all the rest,
First with skilful care they roast it, then draw off as soon as drest.

αὐτὰρ ἐπεὶ παύσαντο πόνου τετύκοντό τε δαῖτα,
δαίνυντ', οὐδέ τι θυμὸς ἐδεύετο δαιτὸς ἐΐσης.
αὐτὰρ ἐπεὶ πόσιος καὶ ἐδητύος ἐξ ἔρον ἕντο,
κοῦροι μὲν κρητῆρας ἐπεστέψαντο ποτοῖο,
νώμησαν δ' ἄρα πᾶσιν ἐπαρξάμενοι δεπάεσσιν,
οἱ δὲ πανημέριοι μολπῇ θεὸν ἱλάσκοντο,
καλὸν ἀείδοντες παιήονα, κοῦροι Ἀχαιῶν,
μέλποντες Ἑκάεργον· ὁ δὲ φρένα τέρπετ' ἀκούων.
Ἦμος δ' ἠέλιος κατέδυ καὶ ἐπὶ κνέφας ἦλθεν,
δὴ τότε κοιμήσαντο παρὰ πρυμνήσια νηός.
ἦμος δ' ἠριγένεια φάνη ῥοδοδάκτυλος Ἠώς,
καὶ τότ' ἔπειτ' ἀνάγοντο μετὰ στρατὸν εὐρὺν Ἀχαιῶν·
τοῖσιν δ' ἴκμενον οὖρον ἵει ἑκάεργος Ἀπόλλων.
οἱ δ' ἱστὸν στήσαντ' ἀνά θ' ἱστία λευκὰ πέτασσαν·
ἐν δ' ἄνεμος πρῆσεν μέσον ἱστίον, ἀμφὶ δὲ κῦμα
στείρῃ πορφύρεον μεγάλ' ἴαχε νηὸς ἰούσης·
ἡ δ' ἔθεεν κατὰ κῦμα διαπρήσσουσα κέλευθον.
αὐτὰρ ἐπεί ῥ' ἵκοντο κατὰ στρατὸν εὐρὺν Ἀχαιῶν,
νῆα μὲν οἵγε μέλαιναν ἐπ' ἠπείροιο ἔρυσσαν
ὑψοῦ ἐπὶ ψαμάθοις, ὑπὸ δ' ἕρματα μακρὰ τάνυσσαν·
αὐτοὶ δ' ἐσκίδναντο κατὰ κλισίας τε νέας τε.
Αὐτὰρ ὁ μήνιε νηυσὶ παρήμενος ὠκυπόροισιν,
διογενὴς Πηλέος υἱός, πόδας ὠκὺς Ἀχιλλεύς·
οὔτε ποτ' εἰς ἀγορὴν πωλέσκετο κυδιάνειραν
οὔτε ποτ' ἐς πόλεμον, ἀλλὰ φθινύθεσκε φίλον κῆρ

When the meal was set, their labour well fulfilled at length they ceast;
Neighbour sharing all with neighbour, lacked not now the social feast.
But when thirst with hunger vanished, then the youths in order due
Crown for all the foaming goblet, and again their round renew.
So the sons of the Achaians all the livelong day employ,
Soothing with melodious paians Him that can from far destroy;
All day long they sang; Apollo heard them sing, and heard with joy.
When the blazing sun had sunken, and the earth around was dark,
Then they slept beside the stern-ropes of the swiftly-faring bark.
But when morning rosy-fingered early dawned upon the coast,
Then they set to sea, returning to the great Achaian host.
Worker from afar, Apollo sped them with a toward gale.
Then they rigged the mast, and featly set aloft the gleaming sail,
Saw it belly to the wind, and heard the wave's exulting boom
Round the bulwarks of the vessel, as she ran careering home.
So when they had made their voyage to the great Achaian host,
Then they hauled the sable galley high and dry upon the coast,
Propped her strongly, and dispersèd each to his appointed post.
But the royal son of Peleus by the winged vessels sate
Ever storming, neither came he to the glory-crowned debate,
Nor to battle; but he wasted, and his heart was dying out,

αὖθι μένων, ποθέεσκε δ' ἀϋτήν τε πτόλεμόν τε.
'Αλλ' ὅτε δή ῥ' ἐκ τοῖο δυωδεκάτη γένετ' ἠώς,
καὶ τότε δὴ πρὸς Ὄλυμπον ἴσαν θεοὶ αἰὲν ἐόντες
πάντες ἅμα, Ζεὺς δ' ἦρχε. Θέτις δ' οὐ λήθετ' ἐφετμέων
παιδὸς ἑοῦ, ἀλλ' ἥγ' ἀνεδύσατο κῦμα θαλάσσης,
ἠερίη δ' ἀνέβη μέγαν οὐρανὸν Οὔλυμπόν τε.
εὗρεν δ' εὐρύοπα Κρονίδην ἄτερ ἥμενον ἄλλων
ἀκροτάτῃ κορυφῇ πολυδειράδος Οὐλύμποιο.
καί ῥα πάροιθ' αὐτοῖο καθέζετο καὶ λάβε γούνων
σκαιῇ, δεξιτερῇ δ' ἄρ' ὑπ' ἀνθερεῶνος ἑλοῦσα
λισσομένη προσέειπε Δία Κρονίωνα ἄνακτα·
"Ζεῦ πάτερ, εἴποτε δή σε μετ' ἀθανάτοισιν ὄνησα
ἢ ἔπει ἢ ἔργῳ, τόδε μοι κρήηνον ἐέλδωρ·
τίμησόν μοι υἱόν, ὃς ὠκυμορώτατος ἄλλων
ἔπλετ'· ἀτάρ μιν νῦν γε ἄναξ ἀνδρῶν 'Αγαμέμνων
ἠτίμησεν· ἑλὼν γὰρ ἔχει γέρας, αὐτὸς ἀπούρας.
ἀλλὰ σύ πέρ μιν τῖσον, 'Ολύμπιε μητιέτα Ζεῦ·
τόφρα δ' ἐπὶ Τρώεσσι τίθει κράτος, ὄφρ' ἂν 'Αχαιοὶ
υἱὸν ἐμὸν τίσωσιν, ὀφέλλωσίν τέ ἑ τιμῇ."
Ὣς φάτο· τὴν δ' οὔτι προσέφη νεφεληγερέτα Ζεύς,
ἀλλ' ἀκέων δὴν ἧστο. Θέτις δ' ὡς ἥψατο γούνων,
ὣς ἔχετ' ἐμπεφυυῖα, καὶ εἴρετο δεύτερον αὖτις·
"Νημερτὲς μὲν δή μοι ὑπόσχεο καὶ κατάνευσον,
ἢ ἀπόειπ', ἐπεὶ οὔ τοι ἔπι δέος, ὄφρ' εὖ εἰδῶ
ὅσσον ἐγὼ μετὰ πᾶσιν ἀτιμοτάτη θεός εἰμι."

As he staid apart, and yearnèd for the onset and the shout.

Time past on, eleven daysprings. With the twelfth, the gods on high,
Zeus their leader, marched in order to Olympus in the sky.
Then from out the waters, Thetis, mindful of her son's behest,
Clad in vapour, scaled high heaven, and the mighty mountain-breast.
Where, apart from every other, Zeus far-thunderer sate enthroned,
On the highest top she found him of Olympus many-coned;
Down she sate before Kronīon, and the lord in prayer addressed,
With her left his knees encircling, while the right his chin caressed.

"Father Zeus, among immortals, if by deed, or if by word,
I have ever done thee service, then, let this my prayer be heard;
Honour Thou my son: Thou know'st him, shortest-lived of all that live;
Him Atrides, lord of heroes, now of honour doth deprive,
For he robbed his prize, and holds it. Whom despite, Olympian Lord!
Counsellor! regard mine offspring, and to Troy the palm award,
Till the host in honour hold him, hold him more than ever great."

Zeus that drives the clouds of heaven, when she ended, silent sate,
Silent long abode. But Thetis, as upon his knees she hung,
So again she questioned, clinging closer than before she clung.

"Either grant it, and confirm it with the nod that all commands,
Or deny; that I may know, (for 'tis not fear that binds thy hands,)
How among Immortals Thetis last and least in honour stands."

Τὴν δὲ μέγ' ὀχθήσας προσέφη νεφεληγερέτα Ζεύς·
"ἦ δὴ λοίγια ἔργ', ὅτε μ' ἐχθοδοπῆσαι ἐφήσεις
Ἥρῃ, ὅτ' ἄν μ' ἐρέθῃσιν ὀνειδείοις ἐπέεσσιν.
ἡ δὲ καὶ αὔτως μ' αἰὲν ἐν ἀθανάτοισι θεοῖσιν
νεικεῖ, καί τέ μέ φησι μάχῃ Τρώεσσιν ἀρήγειν.
ἀλλὰ σὺ μὲν νῦν αὖτις ἀπόστιχε, μή σε νοήσῃ
Ἥρη· ἐμοὶ δέ κε ταῦτα μελήσεται, ὄφρα τελέσσω.
εἰ δ' ἄγε τοι κεφαλῇ κατανεύσομαι, ὄφρα πεποίθῃς·
τοῦτο γὰρ ἐξ ἐμέθεν γε μετ' ἀθανάτοισι μέγιστον
τέκμωρ· οὐ γὰρ ἐμὸν παλινάγρετον οὐδ' ἀπατηλὸν
οὐδ' ἀτελεύτητον, ὅ τι κεν κεφαλῇ κατανεύσω."
Ἦ, καὶ κυανέῃσιν ἐπ' ὀφρύσι νεῦσε Κρονίων·
ἀμβρόσιαι δ' ἄρα χαῖται ἐπεῤῥώσαντο ἄνακτος
κρατὸς ἀπ' ἀθανάτοιο· μέγαν δ' ἐλέλιξεν Ὄλυμπον.
Τώγ' ὣς βουλεύσαντε διέτμαγεν· ἡ μὲν ἔπειτα
εἰς ἅλα ἆλτο βαθεῖαν ἀπ' αἰγλήεντος Ὀλύμπου,
Ζεὺς δὲ ἑὸν πρὸς δῶμα. θεοὶ δ' ἅμα πάντες ἀνέσταν
ἐξ ἑδέων, σφοῦ πατρὸς ἐναντίον· οὐδέ τις ἔτλη
μεῖναι ἐπερχόμενον, ἀλλ' ἀντίοι ἔσταν ἅπαντες.
ὣς ὁ μὲν ἔνθα καθέζετ' ἐπὶ θρόνου· οὐδέ μιν Ἥρη
ἠγνοίησεν ἰδοῦσ,' ὅτι οἱ συμφράσσατο βουλὰς
ἀργυρόπεζα Θέτις, θυγάτηρ ἁλίοιο γέροντος.
αὐτίκα κερτομίοισι Δία Κρονίωνα προσηύδα·
"Τίς δ' αὖ τοι, δολομῆτα, θεῶν συμφράσσατο βουλάς;
αἰεί τοι φίλον ἐστιν, ἐμεῦ ἀπονόσφιν ἐόντα,

Her in mighty dudgeon answered Zeus, the clouds of heaven who drives.
"Nay, 'tis mischief with a vengeance, husbands to embroil with wives:
Well knows Herè how to gall me with reproaches from her tongue;
As it is, she alway taunts me, the immortal gods among,
And affirms I help the Trojans in the fight. But hasten out,
Lest she see thee; leave the matter in my hands to bring about.
Well, so be it; to assure thee, with my head I give the sign:
In the face of the Immortals greater token none is mine:
It recedes not, it misleads not, it shall stand accomplishèd,
Whatsoever I assever with the nodding of my head."

Then beneath his raven eyebrows Zeus Kronion gave the nod,
And the locks ambrosial started from the temples of the god:
Huge Olympus reeled beneath him, root and summit, rock and sod.

So they two, their counsel taken, parted: to the unfathomed sea
She from bright Olympus wended, to his own high palace he.
All the gods arose revering, in the presence of their sire;
None presumed unmoved to meet him, none of all th' immortal choir.
On his throne he sate before them. Nor did Herè need be told
That the silver-footed Thetis, daughter of the sea-god old
Had been scheming with Kronīon; so with stinging words she spake.

"Now with which of the Immortals, Trickster, didst thou counsel take?
Thou dost ever hide thy meaning, plotted in the dark, from me;

κρυπτάδια φρονέοντα δικαζέμεν· οὐδέ τί πώ μοι
πρόφρων τέτληκας εἰπεῖν ἔπος ὅττι νοήσῃς."
Τὴν δ' ἠμείβετ' ἔπειτα πατὴρ ἀνδρῶν τε θεῶν τε
"Ἥρη, μὴ δὴ πάντας ἐμοὺς ἐπιέλπεο μύθους
εἰδήσειν· χαλεποί τοι ἔσοντ' ἀλόχῳ περ ἐούσῃ.
ἀλλ' ὃν μέν κ' ἐπιεικὲς ἀκουέμεν, οὔτις ἔπειτα
οὔτε θεῶν πρότερος τόνγ' εἴσεται οὔτ' ἀνθρώπων·
ὃν δέ κ' ἐγὼν ἀπάνευθε θεῶν ἐθέλωμι νοῆσαι,
μή τι σὺ ταῦτα ἕκαστα διείρεο μηδὲ μετάλλα."
Τὸν δ' ἠμείβετ' ἔπειτα βοῶπις πότνια Ἥρη
"αἰνότατε Κρονίδη, ποῖον τὸν μῦθον ἔειπες;
καὶ λίην σε πάρος γ' οὔτ' εἴρομαι οὔτε μεταλλῶ,
ἀλλὰ μάλ' εὔκηλος τὰ φράζεαι ἅσσ' ἐθέλῃσθα.
νῦν δ' αἰνῶς δείδοικα κατὰ φρένα μή σε παρείπῃ
ἀργυρόπεζα Θέτις, θυγάτηρ ἁλίοιο γέροντος·
ἠερίη γὰρ σοίγε παρέζετο καὶ λάβε γούνων·
τῇ σ' ὀΐω κατανεῦσαι ἐτήτυμον ὡς Ἀχιλῆα
τιμήσῃς, ὀλέσῃς δὲ πολέας ἐπὶ νηυσὶν Ἀχαιῶν."
Τὴν δ' ἀπαμειβόμενος προσέφη νεφεληγερέτα Ζεύς
"δαιμονίη, αἰεὶ μὲν ὀΐεαι, οὐδέ σε λήθω·
πρῆξαι δ' ἔμπης οὔτι δυνήσεαι, ἀλλ' ἀπὸ θυμοῦ
μᾶλλον ἐμοὶ ἔσεαι· τὸ δέ τοι καὶ ῥίγιον ἔσται.
εἰ δ' οὕτω τοῦτ' ἐστὶν, ἐμοὶ μέλλει φίλον εἶναι.
ἀλλ' ἀκέουσα κάθησο, ἐμῷ δ' ἐπιπείθεο μύθῳ,
μή νύ τοι οὐ χραίσμωσιν ὅσοι θεοί εἰσ' ἐν Ὀλύμπῳ

Neither once unasked hast told me what Thy stealthy thoughts decree."

Then the Sire of gods and mortals. "Herè, all my deep discourse
Think not thou to know; a labour, though my wife, beyond thy force.
Whatsoever may be spoken, god nor man shall sooner learn;
What apart from these I counsel, pry not, ask not to discern."

Then in turn addressed him Herè, queenly, with full-orbèd eye,
"Offspring dread of ancient Kronos, wherefore this so strange reply?
Never, till to-day, I asked thee, never pried, to learn thy will;
Alway at thine ease thou couldest all that thou wert pleased fulfil.
But to-day, I sorely fear me lest thy wisdom be cajoled
By the silver-footed Thetis, daughter of the sea-god old;
Clad in vapour she came near thee; of thy knees her arm had hold;
And I trow the vow to honour swift Achilles past thy lips,
And to doom full many a Danaan in the host beside the ships."

Zeus that rolls the clouds of heaven, her addressing answered then.
"Moonstruck! thou art ever trowing; never I escape thy ken;
After all, it boots thee nothing; leaves thee of my heart the less;
So thou hast the worser bargain. What, if I the fact confess?
It was done, because I willed it. Hold thy peace: my word obey;
Lest, if I come near, and on thee these unconquered hands I lay,

ἄσσον ἰόνθ', ὅτε κέν τοι ἀάπτους χεῖρας ἐφείω."
῟Ως ἔφατ', ἔδδεισεν δὲ βοῶπις πότνια Ἥρη,
καί ῥ' ἀκέουσα καθῆστο, ἐπιγνάμψασα φίλον κῆρ·
ὤχθησαν δ' ἀνὰ δῶμα Διὸς θεοὶ Οὐρανίωνες.
τοῖσιν δ' Ἥφαιστος κλυτοτέχνης ἦρχ' ἀγορεύειν,
μητρὶ φίλῃ ἐπίηρα φέρων, λευκωλένῳ Ἥρῃ·
"Ἦ δὴ λοίγια ἔργα τάδ' ἔσσεται οὐδ' ἔτ' ἀνεκτά,
εἰ δὴ σφὼ ἕνεκα θνητῶν ἐριδαίνετον ὧδε,
ἐν δὲ θεοῖσι κολῳὸν ἐλαύνετον· οὐδέ τι δαιτὸς
ἐσθλῆς ἔσσεται ἦδος, ἐπεὶ τὰ χερείονα νικᾷ.
μητρὶ δ' ἐγὼ παράφημι, καὶ αὐτῇ περ νοεούσῃ,
πατρὶ φίλῳ ἐπίηρα φέρειν Διί, ὄφρα μὴ αὖτε
νεικείῃσι πατήρ, σὺν δ' ἡμῖν δαῖτα ταράξῃ.
εἴπερ γάρ κ' ἐθέλῃσιν Ὀλύμπιος ἀστεροπητὴς
ἐξ ἑδέων στυφελίξαι· ὁ γὰρ πολὺ φέρτατός ἐστιν.
ἀλλὰ σὺ τόνγ' ἐπέεσσι καθάπτεσθαι μαλακοῖσιν·
αὐτίκ' ἔπειθ' ἵλαος Ὀλύμπιος ἔσσεται ἡμῖν."
῟Ως ἄρ' ἔφη, καὶ ἀναΐξας δέπας ἀμφικύπελλον
μητρὶ φίλῃ ἐν χειρὶ τίθει, καί μιν προσέειπεν·
"Τέτλαθι, μῆτερ ἐμή, καὶ ἀνάσχεο, κηδομένη περ,
μή σε, φίλην περ ἐοῦσαν, ἐν ὀφθαλμοῖσιν ἴδωμαι
θεινομένην, τότε δ' οὔτι δυνήσομαι, ἀχνύμενός περ,
χραισμεῖν· ἀργαλέος γὰρ Ὀλύμπιος ἀντιφέρεσθαι.
ἤδη γάρ με καὶ ἄλλοτ' ἀλεξέμεναι μεμαῶτα
ῥῖψε, ποδὸς τεταγών, ἀπὸ βηλοῦ θεσπεσιοιο·

All the gods that hold Olympus nought avail thee here to-day."
Trembling Herè sate, and silent (queenly with full orbèd eye)
Curbed her inward soul. Resentment vext the gods that rule the sky,
In their Father's hall. Hephaistos, artist famed, with filial plan
Fain to do his mother pleasure, white-armed Herè, next began.
"Truly here is mischief brewing, mischief we can never bear,
If ye twain, for mortals wrangling, strife and din in heav'n prepare.
Vain the pleasure of the banquet, if the part of fools prevail,
Mother! I advise (albeit thine own wisdom never fail),
Do my Father's pleasure; lest with brawling he the gods assail,
And perturb our feast. For what, should Zeus Olympian, flashing light,
Choose to hurl us from our stations? First is he by far in might.
Come, with gentle words beguile him; he will take such words aright."
He had said; and, quickly rising, placed the double-goblet cup
In his mother's hands; then further spake. "Be patient, and bear up
Mother mine, against thy trouble; lest that here, the gods before,
Smit with stripes we sadly see thee, and in vain thy case deplore;
Vain would be our love: Olympian Zeus is hard to cope withal.
How he seized me, when I came to aid thee in that olden brawl,
Caught me by the foot, and hurled me from the gate of heav'n to fall;

πᾶν δ' ἦμαρ φερόμην, ἅμα δ' ἠελίῳ καταδύντι
κάππεσον ἐν Λήμνῳ· ὀλίγος δ' ἔτι θυμὸς ἐνῆεν·
ἔνθα με Σίντιες ἄνδρες ἄφαρ κομίσαντο πεσόντα."
Ὣς φάτο, μείδησεν δὲ θεὰ λευκώλενος Ἥρη,
μειδήσασα δὲ παιδὸς ἐδέξατο χειρὶ κύπελλον.
αὐτὰρ ὁ τοῖς ἄλλοισι θεοῖς ἐνδέξια πᾶσιν
οἰνοχόει, γλυκὺ νέκταρ ἀπὸ κρητῆρος ἀφύσσων.
ἄσβεστος δ' ἄρ' ἐνῶρτο γέλως μακάρεσσι θεοῖσιν,
ὡς ἴδον Ἥφαιστον διὰ δώματα ποιπνύοντα.
Ὣς τότε μὲν πρόπαν ἦμαρ ἐς ἠέλιον καταδύντα
δαίνυντ', οὐδέ τι θυμὸς ἐδεύετο δαιτὸς ἐΐσης,
οὐ μὲν φόρμιγγος περικαλλέος, ἣν ἔχ' Ἀπόλλων,
Μουσάων θ', αἳ ἄειδον ἀμειβόμεναι ὀπὶ καλῇ.
Αὐτὰρ ἐπεὶ κατέδυ λαμπρὸν φάος ἠελίοιο,
οἱ μὲν κακκείοντες ἔβαν οἶκόνδε ἕκαστος,
ἧχι ἑκάστῳ δῶμα περικλυτὸς ἀμφιγυήεις
Ἥφαιστος ποίησεν ἰδυίῃσι πραπίδεσσιν.
Ζεὺς δὲ πρὸς ὃν λέχος ἤϊ' Ὀλύμπιος ἀστεροπητής,
ἔνθα πάρος κοιμᾶθ', ὅτε μιν γλυκὺς ὕπνος ἱκάνοι·
ἔνθα καθεῦδ' ἀναβὰς, παρὰ δὲ χρυσόθρονος Ἥρη.

From the morn I fell, and fell; and only with the close of day
Lighted down in craggy Lemnos: all my life had ebbed away,
But it chanced the men of Sinte picked me up from where I lay.

Thus he spake. On him the goddess, white-armed Herè, softly smiled;
And with hand outstretched, in smiling, took the goblet from her child.
All the gods he deftly serving from the bowl sweet nectar drew,
As from left to right he travelled step by step in order due.
Then among the blest Immortals burst the laughter uncontrolled,
When they saw divine Hephaistos limp along the halls of gold.

So, until the sun's declining, held they on carousing still:
Neither lacked the social dining, nor the lyre's enchanted skill
In the hand of great Apollo, nor the Muses, that rejoice,
While he plays, to pour in answer liquid notes with sweetest voice.

But the blazing sun descended; each to home and rest inclined;
Each to his own mansion wended, mansion fair, for each designed,
That the maimed and famed Hephaistos builded with his skilful mind.
Zeus Olympian, lord of lightning, sought the couch, where many a day
Slumber soft had bound him. Herè golden-throned beside him lay.

1861.

Horace to Lydia.

Od. III. 9.

Horace. Donec gratus eram tibi,
Nec quisquam potior brachia candidæ
Cervici juvenis dabat;
Persarum vigui rege beatior.

Lydia. Donec non aliâ magis
Arsisti, neque erat Lydia post Chloen;
Multi Lydia nominis,
Romanâ vigui clarior Iliâ.

Horace. Me nunc Thressa regit Chloe,
Dulces docta modos, et citharæ sciens;
Pro quâ non metuam mori,
Si parcent animæ fata superstiti.

HOR. While no more welcome arms could twine
Around thy snowy neck, than mine;
Thy smile, thy heart, while I possest,
Not Persia's monarch lived as blest.

LYDIA. While thou didst feel no rival flame,
Nor Lydia next to Chloe came;
O then thy Lydia's echoing name
Excelled e'en Ilia's Roman fame.

HOR. Me now Threïcian Chloe sways,
Skilled in soft lyre and softer lays;
My forfeit life I'll freely give,
So she, my better life, may live.

LYDIA. Me torret face mutuâ
Thurini Calais filius Ornyti;
Pro quo bis patiar mori
Si parcent puero fata superstiti.

HORACE. Quid si prisca redit Venus,
Diductosque jugo cogit aheneo;
Si flava excutitur Chloe,
Rejectæque patet janua Lydiæ?

LYDIA. Quanquam sidere pulchrior
Ille est; tu levior cortice, et improbo
Iracundior Adriâ;
Tecum vivere amem, tecum obeam libens.

LYDIA. The son of Ornytus inspires
My burning breast with mutual fires;
I'll face two several deaths with joy,
So Fate but spare my Thurian boy.

HOR. What, if our ancient love awoke,
And bound us with its golden yoke;
If auburn Chloe I resign,
And Lydia once again be mine?

LYDIA. Though brighter than a star is he,
Thou, rougher than the Adrian sea,
And fickle as light bark; yet I
With thee would live, with thee would die.

1858.

Catullus to Lesbia.

CARM. LI.

ILLE mî par esse deo videtur,
Ille, si fas est, superare divos,
Qui sedens adversus identidem te
Spectat et audit

Dulce ridentem. Misero quod omnes
Eripit sensus mihi; nam simul te,
Lesbia aspexi, nihil est super mî.
* * * *

HIM rival to the gods I place,
  Him loftier yet, if loftier be,
Who, Lesbia, sits before thy face,
  Who listens and who looks on thee;

Thee smiling soft. Yet this delight
  Doth all my sense consign to death;
For when thou dawnest on my sight,
  Ah wretched! flits my labouring breath.*

* By borrowing from the beautiful Ode of Sappho, which is the prototype if not the original of Catullus, I have filled up the gap, in the sense as well as in the metre, which the Latin presents to us. The first stanza of the Greek closes thus—

βροχεως με φωνᾶς
οὐδὲν ἔτ' ἴκει·

Lingua sed torpet: tenuis sub artus
Flamma dimanat: sonitu suopte
Tintinant aures; geminâ teguntur
Lumina nocte.

Otium, Catulle, tibi molestum est;
Otio exultas, nimiumque gestis:
Otium et reges prius, et beatas
Perdidit urbes.

My tongue is palsied. Subtly hid
  Fire creeps me through from limb to limb:
My loud ears tingle all unbid:
  Twin clouds of night mine eyes bedim.

Ease is thy plague; ease makes thee void,
  Catullus, with these vacant hours,
And wanton: ease, that hath destroyed
  Great kings, and states with all their powers.

1859.

Horace to Pyrrha.

Od. I. 5.

Quis multâ gracilis te puer in rosâ
Perfusus liquidis urget odoribus
Grato, Pyrrha sub antro?
Cui flavam religas comam

Simplex munditiis? Heu quoties fidem
Mutatosque deos flebit, et aspera
Nigris æquora ventis
Emirabitur insolens,

Qui nunc te fruitur credulus aureâ,
Qui semper vacuam, semper amabilem
Sperat, nescius auræ
Fallacis. Miseri, quibus

Intentata nites. Me tabulâ sacer
Votivâ paries indicat uvida
Vestimenta potenti
Suspendisse maris deo.

WHAT scented stripling, Pyrrha, wooes thee now
  In pleasant cavern, all with roses fair?
For whom those yellow tresses bindest thou
          With simple care?

Full oft shall he thine altered faith bewail,
  His altered gods; and his unwonted gaze
Shall watch the waters darken to the gale
          In wild amaze.

Who now believing gloats on golden charms;
  Who hopes thee ever kind and ever void;
Nor, hapless! knows the changeful wind's alarms,
          Nor thee, untried.

For me, let Neptune's temple-wall declare
  How, safe-escaped, in votive offering
My dripping garments own, suspended there,
          Him Ocean-king.

1859.

Ugolino.

INFERNO, C. XXXIII. 1—78.

La bocca sollevò dal fiero pasto
Quel peccator, forbendola ai capelli
Del capo ch' egli avea diretro guasto.
Poi cominciò; tu vuoi ch' io rinnovelli
Disperato dolor, che il cuor mi preme
Già pur pensando pria ch' io ne favelli.
Ma se le mie parole esser den seme
Che frutti infamia al traditor ch' io rodo,
Parlare e lagrimar vedrai insieme.
Io non so chi tu se', nè per qual modo
Venuto se' quaggiù; ma Fiorentino
Mi sembri veramente, quand' io t' odo.
Tu dei saper, ch' io fui 'l conte Ugolino;
E questi l' Arcivescovo Ruggieri:
Or ti dirò, perch' io son tal vicino.
Che per l' effetto de' suo' ma' pensieri,
Fidandomi di lui, io fossi preso
E poscia morto, dir non è mestieri.
Però, quel che non puoi avere inteso,
Cioè, come la morte mia fu cruda,
Udirai, e saprai se m' ha offeso.

THE grim offender from his savage feast
Lifted his mouth; and wiped it with the hair
Of th' head unseemly mauled that he released;
Then thus began. "Am I anew to bear
Desperate grief, that weighs my heart adown,
Even as I think on what I shall declare?
Yet, if my words may, as a seed is sown,
Bring shame to the foul traitor that I gnaw,
In weeping I will speak. One all unknown
Thou com'st: unknown, by what decree or law
Thus low thou didst descend: but Florentine
I guess thy race, by what I heard, not saw.
Thou hast to learn, I was Count Ugoline:
He, Roger, hight Archbishop. Now I tell
The cause of this ill neighbourship of mine.
How by his evil thought's effect it fell,
That I, in him confiding, was ensnared
And put to death, thou, all men, know full well.
But what to boot I trow thou hast not heard,
The manner of my death how horrible,
Hear now; and judge, if ill by him I fared.

Breve pertugio dentro dalla muda
La qual per me ha il titol della Fame,
E' n che conviene ancor ch' altri si chiuda,
M' avea mostrato per lo suo forame
Più lune già, quand' io feci 'l mal sonno
Che del futuro mi squarciò 'l velame.
Questi pareva a me maestro e donno
Cacciando il lupo e i lupicini al monte
Perche i Pisan' veder Lucca non ponno.
Con cagne magre, studiose, e conte,
Gualandi con Sismondi e con Lanfranchi
S' avea messi dinanzi dalla fronte.
In picciol corso mi pareano stanchi
Lo padre e i figli, e con l' agute sane
Mi parea lor veder fender li fianchi.
Quand' io fui desto innanzi la dimane,
Pianger sentì' fra 'l sonno i miei figliuoli,
Ch' eran con meco, e dimandar del pane.
Ben se' crudel, se tu già non ti duoli,
Pensando ciò che al mio cuor s' annunziava:
E se non piangi, di chè pianger suoli?
Già eran desti; e l' ora s' appressava
Che 'l cibo ne soleva esser addotto,
E per suo sogno ciascun dubitava.

A narrow orifice within the cell
(Which yet from me, they call the Famine Jail,
And wherein others, after me, must dwell,)
Had shewn me many moons both wax and fail
Through its dim passage, when I slept the sleep
That rent in twain the future's darksome veil.
A mighty lord, He seemed the plain to sweep,
Chasing the wolf and cubs toward the hill
Which Luccan towers from Pisan eyes doth keep.
With dogs high-bred and lean, of eager skill,
By the Gualandi the Sismondi rides,
And the Lanfranchi helps his train to fill.
Too short, too short the wasting strength abides
Of sire or sons: I seemed to see the stroke,
As the keen fangs dug through the weltering sides.
When I the first, ere break of morn, awoke,
I heard my sons moan faintly in their sleep
That with me dwelt, and bread for life invoke.
Oh thou art hard, if careless yet thou keep,
Learning the then sad presage of my thought!
Oh weep for this, if aught can make thee weep.
The wonted hour for victuals to be brought
Was near at hand: they were awake, and stirred;
But each one, for his dream, was vexed with doubt.

Ed io sentì' chiavar l' uscio di sotto
All' orribile torre: ond' io guardai
Nel viso a' mie' figliuoli senza far motto:
Io non piangeva, sì dentro impietrai:
Piangevan elli: ed Anselmuccio mio
Disse: Tu guardi sì, padre; che hai?
Però non lagrimai: nè rispos' io
Tutto quel giorno, nè la notte appresso,
Infin che l' altro Sol nel mondo uscìo.
Come un poco di raggio si fu messo
Nel doloroso carcere, ed io scorsi
Per quattro visi il mio aspetto stesso,
Ambo le mani per dolor mi morsi:
E quei, pensando ch' io 'l fessi per voglia
Di manicar, di subito levorsi,
E disser: Padre, assai ci fia men doglia
Se tu mangi di noi: tu ne vestisti
Queste misere carni, e tu le spoglia.
Quetàmi allor, per non farli più tristi:
Quel dì, e l' altro, stemmo tutti muti:
Ahi dura terra, perchè non t' apristi?
Posciachè fummo al quarto dì venuti,
Gaddo mi si gittò disteso a' piedi,
Dicendo: Padre mio, chè non m' ajuti?

Aye then, the doorway locked beneath I heard
Of that infernal tower: I gazed upon
The faces of my sons without a word.
I wept not; inwardly I turned to stone:
They wept: and first my dearling Anselm said,
"What ails thee, Father? such thy look is grown?"
I shed no tear for this: nor answerèd
All that same day: nor till the night was gone:
At last, another sun was overhead.
Then, as a scanty ray of light there shone
Into the doleful dungeon, and I read
In their four aspects what must be mine own,
I bit both hands for anguish, hard bestead:
But they, misdeeming it was for distress
Of hunger, in a moment rose, and said,
"Feed, Father dear, on us, so we the less
Shall grieve: do thou, who didst our flesh bestow,
Strip off these miserable limbs their dress."
I held my peace; words had but fed their woe.
Mute that day, mute the next, did we abide;
Merciless earth, that didst not yawn below!
But when there came another morning tide
Then Gaddo fell; and, by my feet reclined,
"My Father, wherefore help'st me not?" he cried;

Quivi morì: e, come tu mi vedi,
Vid' io cascar li tre ad uno ad uno,
Tra 'l quinto dì e 'l sesto: ond' io mi diedi
Già cieco a brancolar sopra ciascuno,
E due dì gli chiamai poiche fur morti:
Poscia, più che 'l dolor potè 'l digiuno."
Quand' ebbe detto ciò, con gli occhi torti
Riprese 'l teschio misero co' denti
Che furo all' osso, come d' un can, forti.

And lived no more. I, whom they left behind,
I saw those three fall slowly, one by one,
In the fifth day and sixth: and, now all blind,
I groped about me after every son:
Two days I called upon their names, though dead;
Then, grief was worsted, and the Famine won."
With savage glance awry, when he had said,
He griped anew the wretched scull; his teeth
Sharp as a mastiff's on that caitiff head.

1837.

The Lord's Prayer.

Purgatorio, C. XI. 1—21.

O Padre nostro, che ne' cieli stai,
  Non circoscritto, ma per più amore
  Ch' a' primi effetti di lassù tu hai;
Lodato sia 'l tuo nome e 'l tuo valore
  Da ogni creatura, com' è degno
  Di render grazie al tuo dolce vapore.
Vegna ver noi la pace del tuo regno,
  Che noi ad essa non potem da noi,
  S' ella non vien, con tutto nostro 'ngegno.
Come del suo voler gli angeli tuoi
  Fan sagrificio cantando Osanna,
  Così facciano gli uomini de' suoi.
Da oggi a noi la cotidiana manna,
  Senza la qual per quest' aspro diserto
  A retro va chi più di gir s' affanna.
E come noi lo mal ch' avem sofferto
  Perdoniamo a ciascuno, e tu perdona
  Benigno, e non guardar al nostro merto.
Nostra virtù, che di leggier s' adona,
  Non spermentar con l' antico avversaro,
  Ma libera da lui, che sì la sprona.

O Father ours, that dwellest in the sky,
Not circumscribed, but for Thy love intense
To Thy first Emanations there on high;
Let each and every creature that hath sense
Praise Thee, Thy name, Thy goodness, as 'tis fit
They render thanks for Thy warm effluence.
Thy kingdom come; Thy peace too come with it,
Which, if it come not by Thy gift divine,
Comes not to us by strength of human wit.
As of their wills the angel Powers to Thine,
Chanting Hosanna, render sacrifice;
So may we men our human wills resign.
Each day give daily manna from the skies,
Without the which, in this rough desert place
He backward slides who forward busiest hies.
And as we pardon each to each, efface
And blot away, benign, our heavier debt,
Nor hold our ill deserts before Thy face.
Our virtue, weak and easily beset,
Oh hazard not with the inveterate foe
That vexeth sore; but free us from his net.

1835.

Speech of Piccarda.

PARADISO, c. III. 70—87.

FRATE, la nostra volontà quieta
Virtù di carità; che fa volerne
Sol quel ch' avemo; e d' altro non ci asseta.
Se disiassimo esser più superne
Foran discordi gli nostri disiri
Dal voler di Colui, che qui ne cerne.
Che vedrai non capere in questi giri,
S' essere in caritate è qui necesse,
E se la sua natura ben rimiri.
Anzi è formale ad esto beato esse
Tenersi dentro alla divina voglia,
Perch' una fansi nostre voglie stesse.
Sì che, come noi siam di soglia in soglia
Per questo regno, a tutto 'l regno piace,
Com' allo Re, ch' in suo voler ne 'nvoglia.
In la sua volontade è nostra pace:
Ella è quel mare, al qual tutto si muove
Ciò ch' ella cria, o che Natura face.

Love by his virtue, Brother, hath appeased
    Our several wills: he causeth us to will
    But what we have, all other longings eased.
Did we desire a region loftier still,
    Such our desire were dissonant from His,
    Who bade us each our several stations fill:
A thing impossible in these spheres of bliss
    If whoso dwelleth here, in Love alone
    Must dwell, and if Love's nature well thou wis.
Within the will Divine to set our own
    Is of the essence of this Being blest,
    For that our wills to one with His be grown.
So, as we stand throughout the realms of rest,
    From stage to stage, our pleasure is the King's,
    Whose will our will informs, by Him imprest.
In His Will is our peace. To this all things
    By Him created, or by Nature made,
    As to a central Sea, self-motion brings.

1835.

In Morte di Napoleone.

ODE

DI ALESSANDRO MANZONI.

1.

Ei fu; siccome immobile,
Dato il mortal sospiro,
Stette la spoglia immemore
Orba di tanto spiro,
Così percossa, attonita
La Terra al nunzio sta;
Muta pensando all' ultima
Ora dell' Uom fatale,
Nè sa quando una simile
Orma di piè mortale
La sua cruenta polvere
A calpestar verrà.

ODE

On the Death of Napoleon.

1.

He died; As in the senseless clay
  No stir of life was left,
When, drawn the mortal sigh, it lay
  Of such a soul bereft,
So, at the tidings thunderstruck
  And pensive, Earth remains:
And muses o'er the dying hour
  And o'er the Child of Fate,
Nor knows if ever such a Power
  Again shall desolate
With like deep track of wounds and stains
  Her blood-red plains.

2.

Lui sfolgorante in soglio
Vide il mio genio, e tacque;
Quando con voce assidua
Cadde, risorse, e giacque,
Di mille voci al sonito
Mista la sua non ha;
Vergin di servo encomio,
E di codardo oltraggio;
Sorge or commosso, al subito
Sparir di tanto raggio,
E scioglie all' urna un cantico
Che forse non morrà.

3.

Dall' Alpi alle Piramidi,
Dal Mansanare al Reno,
Di quel securo il fulmine
Tenea dietro al baleno;
Scoppiò da Scilla al Tanai,
Dall' uno al altro mar.
Fu vera gloria? Ai posteri
L' ardua sentenza. Nui
Chiniam la fronte al Massimo
Fattor, che volle in Lui
Del Creator Suo Spirito
Più vasta orma stampar.

2.

Him, blazing from his throne, to see
My soul in silence bore;
When with quick change he fell, and rose,
And fell to rise no more;
Amidst a thousand voices' throng,
Hers went not up on high,
No slavish adulation stored,
No dastard slander poured;
But stirs and wakes, when such a light
Is quenched in sudden night,
And utters o'er his urn a song
That haply shall not die.

3.

From Alp to farthest Pyramid,
From Rhine to Mansanar,
How sure his lightning's flash foretold
His thunderbolts of war!
To Don from Scilla's height they roar,
From North to Southern shore.
And this was glory? After-men,
Judge the dark problem. Low
We to the Mighty Maker bend
The while, Who planned to show
What vaster mould Creative Will
With him could fill.

4.

La procellosa e trepida
Gioja d' un gran disegno,
L' ansia d' un cuor, che indocile
Ferve pensando al regno,
E 'l giunge, e tiene un premio
Ch' era follia sperar,
Tutto ei provò: la gloria
Maggior dopo il periglio,
La fuga, e la vittoria,
La reggia, e 'l triste esiglio,
Due volte nella polvere,
Due volte su gli altar.

5.

Ei si nomò: due secoli,
L' un contro l' altro armato,
Sommessi a lui si volsero
Come aspettando il fato:
Ei fè' silenzio, ed arbitro
S' assise in mezzo a lor;
Ei sparve: e i dì nell' ozio
Chiuse in sì breve sponda,
Segno d' immensa invidia,
E di pietà profonda,
D' inestinguibil' odio,
E d' indomato amor.

4.

The joy, that o'er some brave design
With thrill tumultuous yearns;
The craving of a heart that, wild
With thought of Empire, burns,
And gains, and holds, the prize it seemed
But madness to have dreamed;
He knew all this, and glory too,
By peril heightened, knew,
The Exile's gloom, the Victor's glare,
The palace or the hut his share,
Twice bit the dust, twice scaled in might
The altar's height.

5.

He dawns; two Ages, armèd each
Against the other, stand;
To him they bend, their doom beseech
Submissive from his hand;
He bids be still, and sits betwixt,
The Arbiter of Fate:
He wanes; an islet's bounds inclose
His terrible repose;
Him Envy's far-drawn arrows wound,
Him Pity's gaze profound
Pursues, him Love unconquered, mixt
With deathless Hate.

6.

Come sul capo al naufrago
L' onda s' avvolve, e pesa,
L' onda su cui del misero
Alta pur dianzi e tesa
Scorrea la vista a scernere
Prode remote invan ;
Tal su quell' alma il cumulo
Delle memorie scese ;
Oh ! quante volte ai posteri
Narrar se stesso imprese,
E sulle eterne pagine
Cadde la stanca man !

7.

Oh ! quante volte, al tacito
Morir d' un giorno inerte,
Chinati i rai fulminei,
Le braccia al seu conserte,
Stette, e dei dì che furono
L' assalse il souvenir.
Ei ripensò le mobili
Tende, e i percossi valli,
E il lampo dei manipoli,
E l' onda dei cavalli,
E il concitato imperio,
E il celere obbedir.

6.

As on the shipwrecked mariner
The weltering wave's descent—
The wave, o'er which, a moment since,
For distant shores he bent
And bent in vain, his eager eye;
So on that stricken head
Came whelming down the mighty Past.
How often did his pen
Essay to tell the wondrous tale
For after times and men,
And o'er the lines that could not die
His hand lay dead.

7.

How often, as the listless day
In silence died away,
He stood with lightning eye deprest,
And arms across his breast,
And bygone years, in rushing train,
Smote on his soul amain:
The breezy tents he seemed to see,
And the battering cannon's course,
And the flashing of the infantry,
And the torrent of the horse,
And, obeyed as soon as heard,
Th' ecstatic word.

8.

Ahi! forse a tanto strazio
Cadde lo spirto anelo,
E disperò; ma valida
Venne un man dal cielo,
E in più spirabil aere
Pietosa il trasportò;
E l' avviò su i floridi
Sentier della speranza,
Ai campi eterni, al premio
Che i desiderii avanza,
Ov' è silenzio e tenebre
La gloria che passò.

9.

Bella, immortal, benefica
Fede, ai trionfi avvezza,
Scrivi ancor questo; allegrati:
Che più superba altezza
Al disonor del Golgota
Giammai non si chinò.
Tu dalle stanche ceneri
Sperdi ogni ria parola;
Il Dio, che atterra e suscita,
Che affanna e che consola,
Sulla deserta coltrice
Accanto a lui posò.

8.

Haply, by that wild struggle riven
The panting heart had failed
In cold despair; but help from Heaven
Descended and prevailed,
And raised him up, and pitying bare
Into a genial air,
And oared him on the flowery ways
Of Hope, and bade aspire
To those blest plains, and to the prize
That passes all desire,
Where darkly sinks in silence down
Earth's brief renown.

9.

O fair, O deathless, O benign,
O still victorious Faith,
This triumph reckon too for thine
With joy; for ne'er in Death
A sterner pride hath stooped to woo
The shame of Golgotha:
From his outwearied ashes warn
Each word of wrath and scorn:
The God, that gives or eases pain,
That smites, and lifts again,
On that lone couch, in that dark day,
Beside him lay.

1861.

Der Graf von Habsburg.

Zu Aachen, in seiner Kaiserpracht,
Im alterthümlichen Saale,
Saß König Rudolphs heilige Macht
Beym festlichen Krönungsmahle.
Die Speisen trug der Pfalzgraf des Rheins,
Es schenkte der Böhme des perlenden Weins,
Und alle die Wähler, die Sieben,
Wie der Sterne Chor um die Sonne sich stellt,
Umstanden geschäftig den Herrscher der Welt,
Die Würde des Amtes zu üben.

Und rings erfüllte den hohen Balkon
Das Volk in freud'gem Gedränge;
Laut mischte sich in der Posaunen Ton
Das jauchzende Rufen der Menge;
Denn geendigt nach langem verderblichen Streit
War die kaiserlose, die schreckliche Zeit;
Und ein Richter war wieder auf Erden.
Nicht blind mehr waltet der eiserne Speer,
Nicht fürchtet der Schwache, der Friedliche mehr,
Des Mächtigen Beute zu werden.

The Count of Hapsburgh.

THE ancient hall of Aix was bright;
The Coronation-board beside
Sate King Rodolph's anointed might,
In Kaiser's pomp and pride:
His meat was served by the Palatine,
Bohemia poured the sparkling wine;
The Seven Electors every one
Stood, fast about the wide-world's King,
Each his high function following,
Like the planets round the sun.

The people, in their joyous throng,
The galleries o'er him crowd,
And the wild trumpet's tone prolong
With acclamations loud;
The kingless time is brought to close,
The desperate struggle to repose,
Earth has a Judge again to-day;
No more prevails the iron spear,
Nor the feeble and the peaceful fear
To be the mighty's prey.

Und der Kaiser ergreift den gold'nen Pokal,
Und spricht mit zufriedenen Blicken:
„Wohl glänzet das Fest, wohl pranget das Mahl,
Mein königlich Herz zu entzücken;
Doch den Sänger vermiß' ich, den Bringer der Lust,
Der mit süßem Klang mir bewege die Brust,
Und mit göttlich erhabenen Lehren.
So hab' ich's gehalten von Jugend an,
Und was ich als Ritter gepflegt und gethan,
Nicht will ich's als Kaiser entbehren."

Und sieh! in der Fürsten umgebenden Kreis
Trat der Sänger in langem Talare,
Ihm glänzte die Locke silberweiß,
Gebleicht von der Fülle der Jahre.
„Süßer Wohllaut schläft in der Saiten Gold;
Der Sänger singt von der Minne Sold,
Er preiset das Höchste, das Beste,
Was das Herz sich wünscht, was der Sinn begehrt;
Doch sage, was ist des Kaisers werth
An seinem herrlichsten Feste?"

The Kaiser grasped the golden cup,
And spake with aspect gladdening all;
"Well shews the board, and my heart leaps up,
Well shines the festival:
Yet I miss the Bard that should bring delight.
And stir my breast with music's might,
And teach me with the god-given strain;
From youth I ever held it so,
And what the Knight was used to do
The Kaiser shall retain."

Then forward stepped, amidst the Peers,
In flowing vest the minstrel dight;
His bleachèd looks with length of years
Were gleaming silver-white.
"Sweet music sleeps in the golden strings,
Of love's reward the minstrel sings,
The highest and the best extols
That sense desires, or heart can pray;
But what can beseem the Kaiser, say,
And the crown of festivals?"

„Nicht gebieten werd' ich dem Sänger," spricht
Der Herrscher mit lächelndem Munde,
„Er steht in des größeren Herren Pflicht,
Er gehorcht der gebietenden Stunde:
Wie in den Lüften der Sturmwind saust,
Man weiß nicht, von wannen er kommt und braust,
Wie der Quell aus verborgenen Tiefen.
So des Sängers Lied aus dem Innern schallt,
Und wecket der dunkeln Gefühle Gewalt,
Die im Herzen wunderbar schliefen."

Und der Sänger rasch in die Saiten fällt
Und beginnt sie mächtig zu schlagen:
„Aufs Waidwerk hinaus ritt ein edler Held,
Den flüchtigen Gemsbock zu jagen.
Ihm folgte der Knapp mit dem Jägergeschoß,
Und als er auf seinem stattlichen Roß
In eine Au kommt geritten,
Ein Glöcklein hört er klingen fern,
Ein Priester war's mit dem Leib des Herrn;
Voran kam der Meßner geschritten."

"I will not bind the minstrel's power,"
With smiling lips the Sovran says:
"He serves a higher lord; the hour,
As it prompts him, he obeys:
Like as in air the whirlwind blows,
And we know not whence its blast arose,
Or fountains from the hidden deep;
The minstrel's song from within him springs,
And stirs the dim imaginings
That in his bosom sleep."

And the Bard he falls to the chords apace,
And strikes them with a master's might.
"The chamois o'er the wild to chase,
Went forth a noble Knight.
A varlet with his rifle rode;
A stately steed himself bestrode;
His path across a meadow ran;
But a tinkling bell from far he hears,
And, with the Host, a Priest appears,
Behind his Sacristan.

„Und der Graf zur Erde sich neiget hin,
Das Haupt mit Demuth entblößet,
Zu verehren mit gläubigem Christensinn
Was alle Menschen erlöset,
Ein Bächlein aber rauschte durchs Feld
Von des Gießbachs reißenden Fluthen geschwellt,
Das hemmte der Wanderer Tritte,
Und beyseit' legt jener das Sakrament,
Von den Füßen zieht er die Schuhe behend,
Damit er das Bächlein durchschritte."

„Was schaffst du?" redet der Graf ihn an,
Der ihn verwundert betrachtet.
„Herr, ich walle zu einem sterbenden Mann,
Der nach der Himmelskost schmachtet;
Und da ich mich nahe des Baches Steg,
Da hat ihn der strömende Gießbach hinweg
Im Strudel der Wellen gerissen.
Drum, daß dem Lechzenden werde sein Heil,
So will ich das Wässerlein jetzt in Eil'
Durchwaten mit nackenden Füßen."

"Then straight the Count to earth bows down,
  And bares his head in reverent thought,
With faithful Christian sense to own
  What our redemption bought.
A streamlet ran that field along;
But now, from Giessbach hoarse and strong,
  High-swollen, it stopped the traveller's way:
The Priest he laid the Host aside,
And from his feet the shoes untied,
  To pass without delay.

"'What dost thou?' So the Count began,
  Entranced in wonder as he stood.
'My Lord, I go to a dying man,
  That longs for the heavenly food;
But the plank, across the brook that lay,
The Giessbach's flood hath borne away,
  Whirled in his waves' tumultuous mass;
Yet, lest the soul that yearns to feed
Should famish, through the stream with speed
  My naked feet shall pass.'

„Da setzt ihn der Graf auf sein ritterlich Pferd,
Und reicht ihm die prächtigen Zäume,
Daß er labe den Kranken, der sein begehrt,
Und die heilige Pflicht nicht versäume.
Und er selber auf seines Knappen Thier
Vergnüget noch weiter des Jagens Begier;
Der Andre die Reise vollführet,
Und am nächsten Morgen mit dankendem Blick
Da bringt er dem Grafen sein Roß zurück,
Bescheiden am Zügel geführet."

„Nicht wolle das Gott," rief mit Demuthssinn
Der Graf, „daß zum Streiten und Jagen
Das Roß ich beschritte fürderhin,
Das meinen Schöpfer getragen.
Und magst du's nicht haben zu eig'nem Gewinnst,
So bleibt es gewidmet dem göttlichen Dienst;
Denn ich hab' es dem ja gegeben,
Von dem ich Ehre und irdisches Gut
Zu Lehen trage und Leib und Blut
Und Seele und Athem und Leben."

" He set the Priest on his lordly steed,
  He gave him the embroidered rein,
That he might help the sick man's need,
  Nor holy rite undone remain.
He, mounted in his varlet's place,
Fills full the pleasure of the chase ;
  But the Priest, his work and journey done,
With careful hand and thankful face
Leads back the charger to the place
  Before the morning sun.

" ' Now God forbid,' right humbly cried
  The Count, ' that or for fight or chase
I e'er again the horse bestride
  That bore my Saviour's grace.
And, if for use he may not be thine,
I give him up to use divine ;
  I give my gallant steed to Him,
From whom my honour and earthly good
I hold on loan, my soul and blood,
  My breath, and life, and limb.'

„So mög' auch Gott, der allmächtige Hort,
Der das Flehen der Schwachen erhöret,
Zu Ehren Euch bringen hier und dort,
So wie ihr jetzt ihn geehret.
Ihr seyd ein mächtiger Graf, bekannt
Durch ritterlich Walten im Schweizerland;
Euch blühn sechs liebliche Töchter.
So mögen sie," rief er begeistert aus,
Sechs Kronen euch bringen in euer Haus,
Und glänzen die spät'sten Geschlechter!"

Und mit sinnendem Haupt saß der Kaiser da,
Als dächt' er vergangener Zeiten:
Jetzt, da er dem Sänger ins Auge sah,
Da ergreift ihn der Worte Bedeuten.
Die Züge des Priesters erkennt er schnell,
Und verbirgt der Thränen stürzenden Quell
In des Mantels purpurnen Falten.
Und alles blickte den Kaiser an,
Und erkannte den Grafen, der das gethan,
Und verehrte das göttliche Walten.

" He set the Priest on his lordly steed,
  He gave him the embroidered rein,
That he might help the sick man's need,
  Nor holy rite undone remain.
He, mounted in his varlet's place,
Fills full the pleasure of the chase;
  But the Priest, his work and journey done,
With careful hand and thankful face
Leads back the charger to the place
  Before the morning sun.

" 'Now God forbid,' right humbly cried
  The Count, 'that or for fight or chase
I e'er again the horse bestride
  That bore my Saviour's grace.
And, if for use he may not be thine,
I give him up to use divine;
  I give my gallant steed to Him,
From whom my honour and earthly good
I hold on loan, my soul and blood,
  My breath, and life, and limb.'

German Verses from Der Freischutz.

Und ob die Wolke sie verhülle,
Die Sonne bleibt am Himmelszelt;
Es waltet dort ein heil'ger Wille;
Nicht blindem Zufall dient die Welt;
Das Auge, ewig rein und klar,
Nimmt aller Wesen liebend wahr.

Für mich wird auch der Vater sorgen,
Dem kindlich Herz und Sinn vertraut;
Und wär' dies auch mein letzter Morgen,
Rief mich sein Vater-Wort als Braut,
Sein Auge, ewig rein und klar,
Nimmt meiner auch mit Liebe wahr.

THOUGH wrapt in clouds, yet still, and still
  The stedfast Sun th' empyrean sways;
There, still prevails a holy Will;
  'Tis not blind Chance the world obeys;
The Eye Eternal, pure, and clear,
Regards, and holds all Being dear.

For me too will the Father care,
  Whose heart and soul in Him confide;
And though my last of days it were,
  And though He called me to His side,
His Eye, Eternal, pure, and clear,
Me too regards, and holds me dear.

1845.

Old Rome.

Par. Regained. B. IV.

The city, which thou seest, no other deem
Than great and glorious Rome, queen of the earth,
So far renowned, and with the spoils enriched
Of nations. There the Capitol thou seest
Above the rest lifting his stately head
On the Tarpeian rock, her citadel
Impregnable. And there Mount Palatine,
The imperial palace, compass huge, and high
The structure, skill of noblest architects,
With gilded battlements conspicuous far,
Turrets, and terraces, and glittering spires.
Many a fair edifice besides, more like
Houses of gods. . . . .

Thou may'st behold,
Inside and outside both, pillars and roofs,
Carved work, the hand of famed artificers
In cedar, marble, ivory, or gold.
Thence to the gates cast round thine eye, and see
What conflux issuing forth, or entering in :

Tu cave ne credas aliam quam prospicis urbem
Romuleâ, rerum dominâ; quæ scilicet orbis
Exuviis prædives ovat, numeratque triumphos.
En ubi rupe tuâ, Tarpeî, domus ipsa Tonantis
Sustulit insignem præstanti vertice formam;
Auratasque arces, et inexpugnabile saxum.
Deinde Palatinos colles, ædesque superbi
Principis immanemque premunt fastigia molem:
En turresque apicesque, et propugnacula longis
Conspicienda viis, et lucida despice tecta.
Quin splendens haud rara domus, similisque deorum.

Ecce et marmoreas aurique, eborisque, columnas,
Cælatusque cedro ut ferit ardua sidera vertex,
Extrorsum introrsumque nitens; quæcunque per urbem
Artifices dederint monumenta insignia dextræ.
Nec non et portas circumspice, quæque catervam
Accipiat venientûm, et quæ vomat ædibus undam.

Prætors, pro-consuls to their provinces
Hasting or on return, in robes of state,
Lictors and rods, the ensigns of their power,
Legions and cohorts, turmes of horse and wings,
Or embassies from regions far remote,
In various habits, on the Appian Road,
Or on the Æmilian, some from farthest South,
Syene, and, where the shadow both way falls,
Meroe, Nilotic isle; and, more to West,
The realm of Bocchus to the blackmoor sea,
Dusk faces, with white silken turban wreathed.
All nations now to Rome obedience pay,
To Rome's great Emperor, whose wide domain
In ample territory, wealth, and power,
Civility of manners, arts, and arms
And long renown, thou justly may'st prefer.

En reditus, en regna Duces semota profectos,
Prætoresque, patris trabeâ cinctuque Gabino;
En comites duros, sellæque insignia virgas.
Hinc legio, inde cohors; hinc ala, hinc gestat equestres
Turma virûm phaleras: longinquæ hinc nuntius oræ
Æmiliam orator peragit, sive Appia ducat,
Diversosque habitus, ignotaque jactitat arma.
Ultima quos Afris domus, aut quos porta Syenes,
Torrida quos Meroe stagnantisque accola Nili,
Misit; ubi radiis Sol desuper instat iniquis:
Quos Bocchus ditione potens, quos marmora Mauri
Oceani; albentem gestat frons furva tiaram.
Scilicet imperium tumido maris æquore clausum
Victa reformidat tellus, ac jussa facessit
Principis: Ille etenim cunctos tenet: Illius arma
Prævalida, imperiumque, inconcussasque cohortes
(Idem armis, idem Ille togâ) famamque perennem,
Mansuetosque virûm mores, ingentiaque auri
Pondera, tu primâ neu dedignere coronâ.

1831.

CPSIA information can be obtained
at www.ICGtesting.com
Printed in the USA
LVHW040424110522
718423LV00002B/466

9 783375 003340